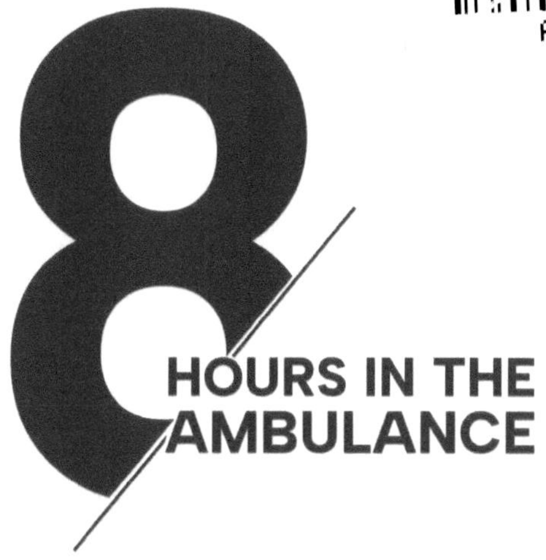

8 HOURS IN THE AMBULANCE

A Fictional Odyssey of Love, Pain, and Resilience

VINOD KUMAR SHARMA

INDIA • SINGAPORE • MALAYSIA

ISBN 979-8-89133-811-1

DEDICATION

This book is dedicated to my dearest wife Laxmi and my grandsons Krish and Avyaan – blessings of God.

FOREWORD

Krish - Grandson:

I didn't have many moments with my Nani, but the few I had are treasures in my heart. Her love and care are etched in my memory.

Avyaan - Grandson:

Dadi, I never had the chance to meet you in person, but I want to thank-you for blessing me with the best mom and dad in the world. Sometimes, I dream about playing with you, listening to bedtime stories, and sharing the best moments of my childhood. Sadly, it remains just a dream. I also wonder why Bua didn't give me the chance to accompany her to the market and insist on buying things out of affection, just like you did even before I was born. I may not have lived with you and Bua, but I listen to your cherished stories day and night from those who remain. I miss you both.

Deepak - Son-in-law:

I've known my mother-in-law for 2 decades, and although she was usually reserved, her thoughtfulness was evident. In all those years, there was hardly a moment when she spoke to me for 20 minutes straight. But my memories of her are sweet, for she knew how to show respect to others.

Ankit - Son:

A son is always close to his mother, and I was no different. Usually, as we grow older and start our own families, we spend less time with our parents. But my mother's values inspired me to prioritise family and spend quality time with them. We used to share meals, play cards, go shopping, and watch movies together. You will forever hold a special place in my heart. I miss you, Mamma.

Priyanka - Daughter-in-law:

Before my marriage, I heard stories from friends and relatives about the challenges of dealing with in-laws, especially mothers-in-law. However, when I met mummy before our wedding, my thoughts began to change, and my apprehensions melted away. She was caring and treated me like her own daughter over time. I believe she was, is, and will always be with me.

Ramesh & Hemlata - Brother and Sister-in-law:

We always regarded her as our mother. I was a village boy, and when I got married, my father asked her to meet Hemlata first and proceed if she agreed. That's the level of respect we had for her. I consider myself lucky to have met her a few days before she passed away. That moment will forever be etched in our hearts.

Ravi & Poonam - Brother and Sister-in-law:

She was the eldest child in our family. From my childhood, I noticed her caring and loving nature toward her siblings, including me. When our mother passed away, Laxmi Jiji took care of all of us. She will always hold a special place in our hearts.

Manoj & Madhu - Brother-in-law and Sister:

Our marriage was marred by problems, and both families disowned us. However, our beloved didi, Laxmi, maintained a relationship with us. Until her last breath, she treated us like her daughter and son-in-law, and we did the same. We will always miss you, didi. We love you.

Devi, Sarla, Pushpa, Daya - Sisters-in-law

Sohan Lal, Brij Lal, Naresh - Brothers-in-law:

Laxmi was the darling of our family because she was the youngest sibling. Despite her youth, we never felt our mother was gone from this world. Laxmi treated all of us with utmost care, and we never felt like our "mayaka" was missing. Some of us had the opportunity to spend months with her, but we all lived with the right to her love and respect.

Deepti & Shashank:

Maa, we met you later in life but recognised you instantly. Paa used to say that in 1983, you lost a child, and in the same year, I was born, making me your daughter. You gave us this incredible feeling. We will never forget that you played the dual role of performing kanyadan and welcoming us into the groom's family. Truly amazing. We miss you, Maa.

All Nephews and Nieces:

We spent time with her on various occasions—some more than others. But our feelings are the same - she was our Mami, Massi, and Bua. She showered us with her love like a mother and a friend. We always felt rightfully at home with her, and she treated us as her own children. We miss you, our best friend.

PREFACE

In the grand theatre of life, they say we're given only one chance - "Zindagi na milegi dobara," they proclaim. But what if I told you, my story unfolds quite differently? Life, for me, isn't a singular journey; it's a series of rebirths within this very lifetime.

My first breath of life came into this world on a crisp November 28th. My parents, the architects of my existence, introduced me to this vast universe. After God, they are the ones I owe my life to. They not only gifted me life but also instilled in me the courage to stand tall and face whatever challenges lay ahead. That, my friends, was my first life.

My second lease on life arrived on a sunny February 24th when I exchanged vows in the sacred institution of marriage. Love, they say, is the elixir of life. It brings meaning and magic to existence. It transforms ordinary days into extraordinary experiences. In love, you find a connection that banishes loneliness. It's the desire to be with your soulmate at all times, in all places. Love breathes life into each day, making it worth living. This second life of mine began with my beautiful wife, a friend, a spiritual soul, a loving mother, and a true companion. It felt like my previous life had ended, and a new chapter had begun. Life had changed since that fateful day, and it was nothing short of magical.

In this new chapter, we navigated life's twists and turns together, savouring every moment. Life, they say, is a journey. And in this journey, time Is the constant traveller, marching forward relentlessly. It's impossible to halt time's progress; all we can do is embrace the journey. And so, 22 years flowed seamlessly by.

During these 22 years, I was never alone. God graced us with 2 noble and caring children, a daughter on March 23rd and a son on April 27th. Life flowed like a peaceful river. It was happy and fulfilling, and I never fathomed that shocks or adversities would come our way. But on November 26th, my world was torn asunder. I had to bid farewell to my dearest daughter, the soul of our family.

It was a bittersweet day, for she was beginning a new chapter with a wonderful partner, a match everyone had hoped for. Even in sadness, there was satisfaction, for everything seemed to be moving smoothly. But fate had other plans.

I entered my third life on November 30th, a day that forever altered the course of my existence. I was nearly broken, for my wife had suffered a paralysing stroke, and everything felt lost. I was in a daze, crying as though life itself had abandoned me. When she regained consciousness after 6 long days in the hospital, it felt as if all my prayers had been answered. I believed I had done something right in my life for the Almighty to hear my pleas and grant me this new life. I thanked God with every breath in my body.

With her unwavering willpower and the grace of God, she made a near-complete recovery, and life resumed its smooth course. I had received a fourth chance at life, and I treasured it.

Life, it seems, often takes us on unexpected journeys. Destiny, an enigmatic force, guides our path. On February 26th, we embarked on a journey to Jaipur to celebrate our marriage anniversary, which fell on the 24th of February. Little did I know that surprises awaited us. My dearest daughter was with us, along with Krish, her son. Then, the following day, a delightful shock awaited us as my best friend, my brother, Manoj, joined our celebration.

We revelled in the joy of the night of February 25th to the 26th at Chowki Dhani, convinced that the universe had showered us with kindness. Little did I know that life's wheel would turn again, subjecting me to pain once more. I pray to God to bless her with health and well-being, for I cannot imagine a life without her. If not, I pray for Him to take me into His eternal embrace.

Love, in its truest form, isn't about becoming someone's perfect match; it's about finding someone who helps you become the best version of yourself.

A JOURNEY OF 34 YEARS UNFOLDING IN 8 HOURS

In the dimly lit hospital reception, tension hung heavy in the air. The clock seemed to tick away relentlessly as we waited for the medical tests to be completed on my wife, Laxmi. It had been two and a half hours, and my thoughts were filled with a mixture of hope and uncertainty.

Our journey to Jaipur had been an unexpected one, a surprise orchestrated by our children for our wedding anniversary. They had wanted to celebrate the occasion in Jaipur, but due to my recent surgery, they had to let me in on the plan, fearing I wouldn't be able to secure leave from work without my knowledge.

But there was another surprise in store for us. As we embarked on our journey from Delhi, we were met on the way by my daughter Shalu and our adorable grandson, Krish. Their unexpected presence brought immense joy and laughter to our trip.

"Shalu, you're here!" I exclaimed. "Why didn't you tell us you were coming with us? We insisted so many times."

"Because, papa, this was meant to be a surprise! And if I had told you, where would the surprise be?" She laughed, and her infectious joy soon spread to all of us. "Thank God you're coming along."

So, there we were, 5 of us, as we started our journey that morning: myself, my wife Laxmi, my son Ankit, my sister-in-law Madhu (Babli), and her daughter Prerna. Shalu's unexpected presence had been a delightful addition to our group.

"Sir, the ambulance is ready!" the driver called out to me, bringing me back from my reverie.

"Oh, yes," I replied, hurrying towards the ward where Shalu was tending to her mother.

"Shalu, please ask the ward boy to bring the stretcher. The ambulance is waiting outside."

"Is everything provided in the ambulance, papa?"

"Yes, everything is ready. Please bring Mama out immediately. We're running late. It's already 3 PM, and we have at least a six-hour journey ahead."

"Sir, the stretcher is ready. Can you please go outside? We're shifting the patient."

"Of course!"

I hurriedly left the room and made my way to the ambulance, my heart heavy, and my steps uncertain. My legs trembled, and I couldn't shake the feeling that I was about to commit a grave mistake. I silently prayed for everything to go smoothly.

"Saab, may I start the vehicle? Is the patient coming?" the driver asked. "Yes, please start it."

As we had set off from Delhi that morning on February 24th, our wedding anniversary, we were in high spirits and a jovial mood.

"Sikandar, please play some old songs on the CD," Laxmi requested the driver.

"No, no, let's listen to some new songs," Prerna chimed in. "Please, Prerna, let's at least hear one old song. If it's not enjoyable, we can change it," I suggested.

"Okay, Maasi."

The melody of an old song filled the air. "Teri aankhon ke siva duniya mein rakha kya hai." We all sang along and shared laughter. I gazed into Laxmi's eyes, which remained as captivating as they had been when we first married 34 years ago.

It felt like just yesterday when she had entered my life with her boundless love and understanding. My first promise to her had been heartfelt:

"I will kiss you and love you with all my heart, and I won't be embarrassed to hold your hand. I'll cherish each day as if it were our last, and at the end of our lives, you won't regret having me as your companion. You are the sunshine in my morning, the song in my heart, and the reason for my courage. You are the mother of my children and the air that gives me life, my trusted friend, my heart, my soul, my wife. My life is beautiful because of you.

I love you deeply, and all that is good in this world is because of you. In return, my love, I ask for one promise from you—that you'll be my companion until my last breath." She had kept that promise to this day.

I was lost in these memories, celebrating our wedding anniversary as we travelled to Jaipur.

"Massad, please ask the driver to switch to new songs. Prerna insists. Enough of the old songs, please, Massad, ask him," Shalu requested.

"Yes, yes, Sikandar, please play some new songs for the kids now."

"Are you feeling hungry, papa?" Shalu asked.

"Oh, yes, let's stop at a good dhaba (roadside eatery) and have lunch. Can't we eat in the ambulance?" Shalu inquired.

"No, dear. We should sit at a proper place, have our lunch, and take some rest," I replied.

"Okay, okay," Shalu agreed.

"Saab, the ambulance is ready, and all the necessary items are provided," the driver informed us.

I snapped back to the present and found myself in the hospital.

"Right, I'll accompany Laxmi," I said. "Shall I also come in the ambulance, Jijaji?" Babli asked. I didn't respond. We both settled into the ambulance as it began its journey back to the Delhi hospital. The rest of the group followed us in an Innova, which we had used to reach Jaipur.

"Why are you sitting, dear? Please lie down," I suggested to Laxmi.

"I can't, I feel nauseous when I lie down on the stretcher inside the ambulance," Laxmi replied. "Okay, do whatever makes you comfortable."

Inside the ambulance, silence enveloped us for half an hour. Each of us was lost in our thoughts, contemplating the stark contrast between our expectations when we set out for Jaipur and the reality that had unfolded.

Negative thoughts gnawed at our minds. What would happen now? This was a part of life, but when your beloved is in pain, restlessness prevails, and only apprehensions fill your thoughts. However, we had no choice but to wait patiently as we made our way back to Delhi.

Just as a surfer doesn't walk away from the ocean or sulk when missing a wave, we too had to keep faith that life's opportunities were like waves, with more waiting to come our way.

Under the vast expanse of the open road, our journey stretched before us, an uncertain path through life's unpredictable waves. It was a day like any other, but little did we know that destiny was poised to hurl us into a tempest, testing our mettle and love.

"Just keep yourself available and be ready to catch your next wave - it's coming any moment!" I whispered to myself as we sped along the highway towards an uncertain future. To understand that problems are teachers is to remain fearless. But was it so easy? Not at all.

"Didi, please keep your head on my lap," Babli implored. "By that way, you will remain seated and not feel nauseous."

"Please come, I want to sit! I am causing you so much trouble, I know," she murmured, her voice heavy with guilt. "Also, all your plans got spoiled."

"Will you shut your mouth, didi, and sit quietly?" I urged, trying to comfort her.

"Are you still feeling nauseous?" I asked with genuine concern.

"No, now I'm feeling much more comfortable," she replied.

"Then sit down. Mind your fractured leg too," I attempted to lighten the atmosphere, masking my own mounting stress.

But in reality, I was overwhelmed. What would happen now? Our lives had become a whirlwind, all revolving around Laxmi. If she remained bedridden, what would we do? It was the most pressing and critical question plaguing our minds at that moment. The anguish my beloved wife endured was unbearable.

Oh God! What had happened?

"We need to stop for food. We're all famished," I suggested as our Innova pulled up at a roadside dhaba, on our way from Delhi to Jaipur.

"Anyone for tea, please?" I inquired.

"All of us will have tea," Babli declared. "No, no, I'll have Pepsi," Prerna chimed in. "I'll also have Pepsi," echoed Shalu, Vicky (Ankit), and little Krish.

"Alright, the waiter is coming. Just tell him what you need."

Laxmi opened a box filled with puris and aloo ki sabzi, along with some chutney.

We ordered Dal Tadka, cold drinks, and tea, and started our meal without delay, our laughter filling the air as we shared stories and jokes.

After an hour at the dhaba, we continued our journey, with music filling the air. The battle between old and new songs ensued.

Ultimately, the classics prevailed as an old, timeless song filled the car. "Na tum humein jaano, na hum tumhein jaanein, magar lagta hai kuchh aisa mera humdum mil gaya."

I disappeared into the melody, reminiscing about the day we first met after our wedding. We were practically strangers at that time, having barely known each other before the wedding. Yet, when I saw her, it was as if I had known her for lifetimes, her face so familiar that it startled me.

In those days, there were no cell phones or communication before marriage. We met briefly on her first day in our home.

"What's your name?" I asked, eager to hear her voice.

No reply.

"Please tell me your name?" I insisted. "Don't you know my name?" she retorted.

"I do, but I want to hear it from you."

"Laxmi," she replied.

"So sweet, as if Goddess Laxmi herself has graced our home. Thank God!" I exclaimed.

She smiled for the first time. "I'm not a goddess; I'm just a simple girl."

At the time of our marriage, she was merely 18, barely out of school, and had been thrust into a world of wedlock. It was destiny, and I was content with it. Our first meeting lasted only 5 minutes, but she didn't feel like a stranger. It is a truth that those we meet in this life are often connected through lifetimes past.

I yearned to spend more time with her, to know her better, but my mother called me away.

"Vinod! Come down immediately." I reluctantly bid Laxmi goodbye, as our house was bustling with preparations for the Jagaran and the reception in the following days.

When you meet your soulmate, the exhaustion fades into insignificance. That was my case.

"Where would you like to go for our honeymoon?" I inquired after the relatives dispersed following the reception.

"I don't know," she replied. I wasn't certain either. We were both young, and convincing our families to let us travel alone was a daunting prospect. Nevertheless, I was determined, and so we went.

We embarked on our honeymoon to Shimla, accompanied by 2 of my friends. A peculiar arrangement, indeed. But it was the only way we could make the journey. I had told my father that a colleague and his wife would be joining us, easing his concerns.

"Jijaji, Jijaji, didi is still feeling nauseous. Please talk to the doctor to see if she can have some medicine," Babli interjected, pulling me from my reverie.

"Ah, what did you say?" I was lost in my memories and took a moment to return to the ambulance.

"Didi isn't feeling well. Can you please talk to the doctor and get some medicine?" Babli repeated.

"Sure," I went to Laxmi and asked her what was wrong. She was truly unwell. She hadn't eaten anything since morning, and it was now about 5 o'clock. This was concerning, especially given her diabetes; not eating could lead to low blood sugar.

"Don't worry. Everything will be alright," I reassured her.

"I'll talk to the doctor and pick up some medicine from a nearby pharmacy," I informed her.

I was deeply distressed by my wife's condition, feeling helpless in the face of her suffering. I prayed fervently that we would reach Delhi soon so that she could receive the medical attention she needed.

I spoke to the doctor in Jaipur, who suggested a medication that might help with her immediate symptoms, at least the nausea.

I returned to her and sat by her side, gently combing her hair with my fingers in an attempt to comfort her. Unsuccessful in concealing my tears, I let them fall silently. Seeing my wife in pain was truly heartbreaking.

"Driver, please stop at a chemist shop on the way," I instructed, having received the doctor's recommendation.

"Babli, please give some orange to your didi," I requested. "No, no, I won't eat anything. I might vomit," Laxmi replied.

"Alright, but please have something. I can't give you medicine on an empty stomach."

"Babli, please give it to her." I handed the orange to Babli, who offered it to Laxmi.

I collected the medicine on the way and handed a tablet to Laxmi.

In the quietude of our shared solitude, Laxmi's illness cast a shadow over our lives, compelling her to remain upright. Her words hung in the air like a fragile thread, as I implored her to rest. "Please take some rest and lie down," I urged.

"No, I can't, because I feel the nausea creeping in when I recline," she responded with a hint of discomfort.

"Alright," I conceded, my heart heavy with concern. I turned my gaze to the heavens, silently beseeching divine intervention for the well-being of my beloved. It was a plea borne out of desperation; the only recourse available in those trying circumstances.

Wisdom, that elusive beacon, whispered to us, urging us to flow with the currents of time, to navigate life's turbulent waters with grace and resilience. It taught us to face challenges without fear, to extract lessons from adversity, and to press onward, forever evolving. Every hurdle, we realised, was but a fleeting moment, and the world around us was in a perpetual state of flux. If we could adapt and remain pliant, we would be equipped to confront any obstacle that lay in our path. Wisdom gifted us courage, the ability to identify obstacles from afar, and the foresight to prepare for their arrival.

As I pondered these profound truths, my thoughts were momentarily interrupted by a memory—a recollection of the day we had exchanged vows. I, a youthful 23, and she, a tender 18, had embarked on our journey into matrimony, hastened by the whims of fate.

"Alright, talk to Ramesh. Why engage with me now that he's gone?" I responded to Laxmi's interruption; my words laced with a tinge of jealousy.

"Oh, are you feeling jealous?" Rita quipped, her eyes sparkling with mischief.

This episode had transpired before the binding commitment of our marriage and had been the catalyst for our early union. Our shared shorthand class had brought us together—Rita, Ramesh, me, Jaspreet Kaur, and Devesh. We hailed from the same neighbourhood and often walked together to class. Yet, it was at a certain juncture on our way home that Rita's unbroken conversation with Ramesh had stirred the embers of jealousy within me.

"Please, talk to Ramesh only," I had implored, attempting to mask my discomfort.

Rita halted abruptly, her expression grave. "Alright, Vinod, if you wish that I speak to no one else in the class, I shall fulfil your wish and speak to only you starting tomorrow."

I chuckled, dismissing her promise. "Come on, Rita, don't make vows you can't keep."

Her gaze remained resolute. "I am serious, Vinod."

"Very well, let's see," I acquiesced, and we resumed our journey home, soon forgetting the incident. It was a time when innocence prevailed.

The following day, Rita spoke to me incessantly on our way to class, as was our custom. Yet, upon our arrival, she greeted no one, not even our teacher—an unusual departure from her routine. I alone comprehended the reason behind this peculiar behaviour, and I was taken aback. Could a girl possess such steadfast determination to honour her promise? I couldn't fathom the depth of her resolve. It raised questions within me—was it merely liking or had love entered the equation? To this day, that distinction eludes me.

Days turned into weeks, and Rita was absent from our class for an extended period, leaving us to speculate. I yearned for her company, our conversations, the spontaneous pauses on our way home to chat endlessly. Her absence was deeply felt.

Then, one fateful day, I crossed paths with her unexpectedly on the street, accompanied by my brother-in-law. My heart leaped at the sight of her.

"Why have you been absent from class?" I inquired eagerly.

"I've been down with fever," she replied weakly.

"Let me feel your forehead," I suggested, eager to gauge her condition.

She extended her hand, and as I reached out, our fingers intertwined in an unexpected handshake. My brother-in-law, unaccustomed to such interactions between a young man and a woman in those times, cast a suspicious glance in my direction. He would later relate this incident to my father, invoking a stern conversation.

"Listen, papa, there's something important I need to discuss," my brother-in-law approached my father with concern.

"What is it?" my father inquired.

My brother-in-law recounted the entire episode, leaving my father perturbed. To him, my potential affection for Rita was a matter of great concern, as such a match would be unthinkable due to the difference in our castes—a paralysing fear for children of that era.

"What's the matter, Vinod?" My father turned his attention to me. "Why are you staying silent? Is what your brother-in-law says true?"

"Nothing, papa," I muttered.

"But he claims that you shook hands with a girl on the road. It's not appropriate."

"It wasn't intentional, papa," I explained.

"Who is she?" my father pressed.

"She's in the same shorthand class as me."

"This doesn't bode well, Vinod. Please be more careful in the future."

"Alright, papa, I will."

My brother-in-law urged my father to find a suitable match for me before the situation escalated. I couldn't express my true sentiments to my father, but I confided in my mother, declaring my reluctance to marry at such a young age.

"I'm not ready for marriage yet, Mataji," I protested.

"Who is forcing you to marry so soon?" she inquired.

"Papa and Jijaji are pressuring me," I confessed.

"I will speak to them," she assured.

"Please, Mataji, do something. I want to explore the world and establish myself before getting married. I need to stand on my own 2 feet first."

She nodded in understanding.

"If Vinod isn't ready for marriage just yet, why are you insisting?" my mother queried.

"Please don't interfere," my father retorted.

"Why shouldn't I? He's my son too, and pressuring him on this sensitive issue isn't right," she argued.

"He has befriended a girl, Brijlalji told me. He shook hands with her on the road."

"He's admitted his mistake and promised not to repeat it," my mother interjected.

"You don't understand. If this continues, we won't be able to show our faces in society."

Tensions simmered in our household, and the future hung in uncertainty, shrouded by the shadow of tradition and societal expectations.

In the depths of my memories, there existed a tale, one woven from the threads of fate and family bonds. It began with my father, a man of resolve and desperation, who would eventually resort to a most unconventional measure to secure my future.

"Get married when I am no longer in this world," he implored, his words hanging heavy in the air. Shocked, I could only remain silent. There was no response to offer, no comforting words to quell his emotions.

Countless girls were considered, their horoscopes scrutinised, and their virtues debated. But then, like a whisper from the distant past, my brother unearthed a name from our family history.

"Jiji," my brother addressed our mother one day in the midst of this matrimonial quest, "there was a woman who used to grace our home on special occasions. A woman of exceptional beauty."

Mother, fondly called Mataji, inquired, "Who do you speak of?"

"She used to accompany Taiji and Anaro Masiji," my brother explained.

"Are you referring to Sheila?" Mother questioned.

"Yes," he affirmed, "She was stunningly beautiful, and she has a daughter who must be of marriageable age now. Perhaps we should reach out to them."

Mataji was unsure of their whereabouts. "I don't know where they are presently," she admitted.

"Why don't you speak to Taiji?" my brother suggested.

"Very well, I shall," was her response.

The trail was cold, a distant memory from days long past. Nonetheless, relentless efforts bore fruit, and the elusive family was located.

With hope in their hearts, my father, brother, and Tauji, a close family friend, journeyed across the Yamuna River to visit Sheila's home. Sheila herself looked at Tauji with a spark of recognition in her eyes, though it had been ages since they last met.

"You remember," Tauji began, "we used to visit Chuna Mandi, Paharganj, on various occasions. We used to celebrate those moments at their home."

"Are you speaking of the lady who had 6 daughters and 2 sons?" Sheila inquired.

"Yes, that's her," Tauji replied, "Do you recall now?"

"It's been so long," she mused.

"You had a daughter back then," my brother ventured, "she must be of marriageable age now."

"She's just turned 18," Sheila disclosed.

"The young man is 23," my brother continued, "if you're willing, we could discuss their match."

"We will consult and get back to you," Sheila agreed.

My brother and father returned home with this promising development.

"Mataji, Tauji has arrived," I informed her.

"Please come in," I added.

Papa and Mataji joined in the drawing room to hear the news.

"They wish to meet Vinod and all of you," Tauji shared.

"That's wonderful news," Mataji exclaimed, "We will consult and make arrangements."

"Let's meet next Sunday at Birla Mandir, around 4 pm," Tauji suggested.

"We'll be there," Mataji confirmed.

Excitement filled the air, but I couldn't share in the joy. I was not prepared for marriage at such a tender age, and my heart was entwined with another – Rita, my dearest friend. Our connection was not love in the romantic sense, for we were still too young to grasp its complexities. Instead, it was a profound friendship.

Nevertheless, the day arrived when I laid eyes upon the girl destined to be my wife, Laxmi. Love at first sight is a concept I never truly believed in until that moment. It wasn't mere physical attraction, but an inexplicable connection, a chemistry that defied explanation. We were drawn together like 2 stars in the night sky.

We married, Laxmi and I, and as I look back, I realise that everything happened for a reason. Without that twist of fate, I might never have found a love as profound as ours. I thank the heavens for this chance.

I've come to believe that love at first sight is more about the chemistry between souls than the physical allure. It's a connection that transcends time and circumstance, a recognition of something deeper than the eye can see.

Life, as we know it, is a blend of joys and sorrows, love and loss. How we navigate this journey is a testament to our character. We can let hardships divide us, or we can use them to fortify our spirits and amplify our capacity for love. We can choose to complain or to serve, to share God's love, and bring a smile to Heaven's face.

My life was incomplete until you entered it. You, my wife, my treasure, a divine gift I can never measure. I cherish the boundless love you bring, knowing that you are a gift from Heaven. I vow to never let frustration taint our love, but to hold you close, showering you with affection. This is no game of chance, but a deep commitment to remain by your side, not just in this life but in every life that follows.

I reminisce about our early days, when we were naive and oblivious to the complexities of life. With time, we grew to understand each other, our bond strengthening. No one could sow discord between us. I recall a particularly amusing incident when we returned from the bus station after bidding farewell to my elder brother and sister-in-law.

"Please open the door," I requested, knocking repeatedly.

Silence.

"Laxmi, please open the door!"

The backstory was that we had gone to see off my brother and sister-in-law after their wedding celebrations in Hissar. Rain had drenched us on the way back, leaving us shivering in the early March chill.

We changed into dry clothes upon our return, but Laxmi locked herself in the bedroom. After about 15 minutes, I ventured to knock, yet she remained asleep, oblivious to my pleas. It was a comical and unforgettable incident.

Life has its moments when we yearn for someone so profoundly that we wish to pull them from our dreams and hold them in our arms. Happiness, I've learned, is reserved for those who have tasted sorrow, for those who have sought and striven, for they alone understand the value of the people who touch their lives.

Lost in these reveries, I was abruptly jolted back to the present by the wailing sirens of an ambulance racing down the road. I returned to reality, though a part of my heart lingered in the past.

In the realm of dreams, where the boundaries of reality blur and the possibilities are as endless as the night sky, I found myself contemplating the essence of life. "Dream what you want to dream; go where you want to go; be what you want to be, because you have only one life and one chance to do all the things you want to do." These words whispered through my mind like a gentle breeze, a reminder of the fleeting nature of existence.

As I drifted in thought, my surroundings faded into obscurity, and there was nothing else but the anticipation of reaching our destination or the reminiscence of moments shared. In those moments of reflection, I found myself embracing empathy, for it is said, "Always put yourself in others' shoes. If you feel that it hurts you, it probably hurts the other person too." And indeed, I could feel the anguish that Laxmi was enduring.

Life, it seemed, was a ceaseless machine, churning out thoughts beyond our control. Yet, amidst the whirlwind of emotions and uncertainty, one thought remained steadfast in the ambulance that rushed us toward an unknown future: how to ease Laxmi's discomfort. The machinery of thoughts did not falter, and before my eyes, the panorama of my life unfurled once more.

"No, I won't wear this dress! What will Mataji say?" Laxmi's protest echoed in my ears. "How will Mataji ever find out?" I replied, my voice a gentle plea. "Please, wear this dress; you will look beautiful in it."

Laxmi, my young bride of just 18, hesitated, her demeanour childlike and innocent. Yet, with persistence, I convinced her to change, assuring her of her beauty in the mirror's reflection.

"See, you are looking so beautiful in this dress!" I exclaimed, my heart swelling with affection. "See in the mirror."

Her cheeks flushed with shyness as she glanced at her reflection. "Please smile, and I'll capture this moment," I urged.

She obliged with a timid smile. "You are too kind," I whispered after taking the photograph.

In the picturesque haven of Shimla, we wove the tapestry of unforgettable moments. Our days were filled with sightseeing and movie dates, our hands entwined, our worries left far behind. Time, elusive as ever, slipped through our fingers during that week of pure bliss as we sought to understand each other better.

But as we journeyed back on the train, a shadow of unease descended upon us. Laxmi, for a moment, sat in silence, her eyes filled with apprehension. "Why are you looking so sad?" I inquired gently.

"We deceived our parents, didn't we?" Laxmi replied, her voice tinged with guilt.

"It's alright," I reassured her, though my own worry gnawed at me. "Please don't dwell on it. We'll find a way to make things right."

"You don't need to worry," Laxmi responded with determination. "I will handle the situation."

As expected, tension hung heavy in the air upon our return. Mataji's demeanour was stern, and the unease was palpable.

"Mataji, what happened?" I ventured to ask.

"Nothing of consequence," she replied cryptically.

"I apologise, Mataji," I offered, my voice tinged with remorse.

"Don't apologise," Mataji admonished. "You did it knowingly."

"What else could we do? You would never have allowed us to go out," I confessed.

"We are not your enemies," Mataji responded, her tone softening. "You both are still learning how to navigate the world outside."

"I know, but we yearned to experience it," I conceded. "I'm sorry, and we won't do it again."

Time passed, and like settling dust, the tension slowly dissipated, leaving behind a semblance of normalcy.

Love, they say, is a gamble, never guaranteeing reciprocation. Yet, in our case, love bloomed in both our hearts like 2 harmonious plants sharing the same pot. It was our understanding that drew us ever closer.

The world outside blurred as I returned to the present, where uncertainty clung to the air like an invisible shroud. Babli's urgent voice pierced through my reverie.

"Jijaji, Jijaji, are you listening?" Babli inquired anxiously. "How much longer until we reach the hospital? Didi is in pain."

"I understand. How far have we come?" I asked the driver. "How much longer?"

"Saab, it will take about 4 hours to reach Delhi," he replied.

"Please, try to rest. It might alleviate the discomfort," I suggested to Laxmi, fully aware of her inability to do so. The relentless journey had taken its toll, and hunger gnawed at her, aggravated by the pain in her ankle.

I sat by her side, cradling her head in my lap, my fingers gently tracing her hair, offering a semblance of comfort. She closed her eyes, attempting to find solace in sleep, but it remained elusive.

"Please, have something," I implored. "No, I don't feel like it," Laxmi replied.

"Please, for the sake of the medication," I urged.

Reluctantly, she acquiesced, and I offered her slices of orange. While I didn't shed tears, the emotions within me ran deep. I longed to bear her pain, to shoulder her burdens, but the limitations of reality held me captive.

Life, it seemed, was a constant battlefield, with conflicts both small and significant. In those moments, I pondered the wisdom of choosing our battles, preserving our energy for the true challenges that lay ahead.

It wasn't the busyness of life that drained us; it was the relentless churn of our thoughts. The key to avoiding exhaustion lay in staying focused, maintaining a sense of calm, and not allowing ourselves to be consumed by problems. It was easier said than done, especially when the one you loved lay in pain, and your heart was entangled in the turmoil.

Life often throws obstacles in our path, thwarting our aspirations and breeding negativity. In the face of such adversity, some would wage war, consumed by anger and bitterness. Yet, life held unforeseen surprises, dreams that transcended the boundaries of imagination. Such was the tale of Babli, a story waiting to unfold.

In the heart of our family's tale, there resides Babli, my wife's sister, a soul brimming with kindness, always ready to shoulder the burdens of crisis without a second thought. She was our saviour. Much the same was the nature of her husband, Manoj. The story of how they drew close to us is etched in my memory.

Babli was but a tender bud in the bouquet of our matrimony. She was too young to comprehend the intricacies of wedlock. When Laxmi, my beloved wife, tied the knot at the tender age of 18, her siblings were but children. Yet, all of them held a special place in my heart, drawn by my welcoming nature that encouraged everyone to confide in me.

Four to 5 years into our marriage, Babli found herself staying at our home for a spell. One day, she approached me with a timid question.

"Jijaji," she began hesitantly, "may I seek your counsel on something?"

"Of course, Babli," I replied. "You may ask me anything."

With a hint of reluctance, she asked, "Is it possible for a boy and a girl of different castes to marry?"

"It depends, Babli," I replied. "What's troubling you?"

She hesitated for a moment, then confessed, "It's about one of my friends. She's fallen in love with a Punjabi boy."

"What caste is your friend?" I inquired.

"They are Gargs," she replied.

"I fear the Gargs may not be receptive to a Punjabi alliance," I mused.

"Is there no solution?" she asked, her distress evident.

"Why are you so concerned about your friend's predicament?" I questioned her.

She remained silent and offered no explanation.

"Please advise your friend to focus on her studies for now," I suggested. "Marriage need not be her immediate concern."

"Alright, I will do that," she responded.

I was taken aback by the gravity of her question, for she was hardly 16 or 17 at the time. Several months later, she broached the same subject, revealing that her friend was deeply in love and yearned to marry the Punjabi boy. I explained that such a union was only possible with the consent of both sets of parents. Babli fell silent again, her worry palpable.

"What's troubling you, Babli?" I inquired. "Is this about you?"

A deep, uneasy silence followed. It was then that I realised the truth: Babli herself was in love with a Punjabi boy.

"No, it's impossible," I stated firmly. But her tears flowed freely as she leaned her head upon my shoulder and implored, "I can't live without him, Jijaji. Please, do something!"

I was shocked by the revelation. Such a young girl, entangled in a love affair with someone from a different caste.

"Who is this boy? What's his name? Do I know him?" I asked.

"Yes, you do. His name is Manoj, a friend of Bhai, and he lives just across from our house," she confessed.

I knew then that her father held conservative views and would never approve of this union. I had met Manoj on several occasions while visiting Babli's family.

"Let me think about it. I'll talk to your father," I offered.

"No, Jijaji, please don't. He will confine me to our home and never let me out," Babli replied.

I decided to discuss the matter with my wife, Laxmi.

"Laxmi, I need to tell you something," I began.

"What is it? Why do you seem so serious?" she inquired.

"Babli is in love with a Punjabi boy," I revealed.

"What are you saying? Babli can't be like this," she exclaimed in disbelief.

"But it's true; she told me herself," I replied.

"Are you joking?" Laxmi remained in a state of shock, unable to utter a word.

We were already parents to a little girl named Shalu by then, and we understood the consequences of broaching this alliance with her parents.

"Why didn't you talk to me before discussing it with Jijaji?" Laxmi asked Babli when they met a few days later.

"Didi, I was afraid and didn't know how to tell you," Babli replied.

"You realise what could happen now, don't you? You're diving into this without understanding the consequences," Laxmi scolded her.

The question that weighed on us was whether or not to approach Bauji, Babli's father. But before that, we needed to ascertain whether Manoj was equally committed to this relationship.

"Manoj, please tell me your intentions," I asked him during one of my visits to Babli's home.

"Yes, Jijaji, I want to marry Babli," he responded, addressing me as Jijaji and Laxmi as didi, as he was a friend of Laxmi's brother Ravi.

"Have you spoken to your parents about this?" I inquired.

"No," he admitted.

"How can we proceed then? Shall I speak to them?" I offered.

He remained as still as a statue.

How could I approach the conservative parents of a girl to propose a marriage to a Punjabi boy when I knew it was nearly impossible? I couldn't even muster the courage to discuss it with my own parents, who held equally conservative views.

"Jijaji, please give didi some water. She's thirsty, and her head is on my lap," Babli interrupted my thoughts. I snapped back to the present.

"Of course, I'll get her some water," I replied as I carefully brought a glass to Laxmi's lips.

"Are you still in pain?" I asked her.

It was a foolish question, for I knew well that her suffering could not be eased through mere conversation. There were situations in life that we had to endure without allowing them to consume us completely. If we surrendered to the tempest, we would lose control of our life's course. However, we had no control over the circumstances themselves, nor did we possess the solutions.

"Jijaji, please help us," Babli implored during one of my visits to her home. I found myself revisiting Babli's story once more.

"How can I help when the boy is too shy to approach his parents?" I replied. "If I speak to Bauji (her father), and the boy cannot find his voice, it will be an embarrassing situation."

Tears streamed down her face as she cried, "I can't live without him. Please, do something."

"Please don't cry, I will try my level best," I replied, my voice laced with determination.

I leaned in closer to Manoj one day, desperation in my eyes as I implored, "Manoj, please talk to your parents and help me speak to Bauji."

Manoj nodded solemnly. "Sure, I will talk to them in a day or 2," he assured me.

I snapped back to the present when I heard Laxmi's desperate cries. "Aah, I'm feeling nauseous, please open the window," she pleaded.

Concern etched across my face; I moved my fingers gently through her hair. "What happened? You've already taken the tablet."

Laxmi's voice trembled as she responded, "I'm still feeling nauseous."

I hurriedly opened the window, but nothing came out. She hadn't been able to eat anything since morning, and we felt utterly helpless.

"How much time will it take to reach?" I asked the driver, desperation creeping into my voice.

"About 2 hours if there's no traffic," he replied calmly.

"Oh God, please help," I exclaimed, tears welling up in my eyes. I felt an overwhelming sense of helplessness, knowing we had no control over the situation.

Laxmi shifted, seeking comfort, and rested her head on Babli's lap.

"Babli, you must be tired. Let me offer my lap so you can rest," I suggested.

"No, I'm fine," Babli replied, her unwavering support evident.

I couldn't help but reflect on the sacrifices we make for our loved ones in times of trouble, a heavy sigh escaping me. My thoughts drifted back to Babli's journey.

Finally, Manoj delivered the welcome news that his parents had agreed, after much persuasion. This marked a significant step forward, as I knew that if I could speak to Bauji, one obstacle would be cleared. But I also understood that it wouldn't be easy.

"Bauji, there's something important I'd like to discuss," I murmured during our next visit to their home.

Bauji looked at me, concern in his eyes. "Tell me, beta, is there a problem?"

"No, there's no problem," I assured him. "I want to talk to you about Babli."

His curiosity piqued; he leaned forward. "What has she done?"

"Nothing, but she's in love with a boy," I replied.

In an instant, he rose from his chair, his voice filled with disbelief. "What are you talking about?"

"Babli, come here," he called out loudly.

"Please, Bauji, sit down and listen carefully," I implored.

He was trembling with excitement, visibly agitated. I knew this would be his initial reaction, but I worried about how he'd respond when he learned that the boy was a Punjabi and a neighbour. Would his blood pressure spike? Would he fall ill? The situation felt tense and precarious.

Babli entered, trembling, and fell silent.

"Who is this boy? Tell me immediately! How dare you?" Bauji's voice remained raised, and he stood again.

I managed to get him to sit down and asked Babli to do the same.

Everyone in the room stared at me, astonished and curious, except for Laxmi, who was already aware of everything.

"You know this boy. He's your neighbour, Manoj," I began cautiously.

"Manoj!" Bauji exclaimed, his eyes wide with surprise. "I can't believe it. He's Punjabi. This can't happen while I'm alive. How will society react?"

I asked everyone else in the room to leave, including Babli, and only Laxmi, her mother, and I remained.

"Bauji, please try to understand," I pleaded. "Both of them are adults. You might not be ready for this alliance now because he's Punjabi, and you're worried about society's reaction. But what if they run away and get married in court? How will society react then? Which situation is better getting your daughter married across castes, or the latter?"

Bauji looked at my face, his head in his hands.

"Take your time to decide," I reassured him, placing my hand on his shoulder. "Whatever you decide, we will accept it."

He appeared restless, and I felt the same. The situation was complex, and I realised that as parents, we couldn't force our children's decisions.

"I need to sit down for a while," Laxmi requested.

I snapped out of my reverie and gently helped her sit down, my words offering reassurance, even though I, too, had doubts about my own counsel. But in such circumstances, there was little else we could do.

"How much longer until we reach Delhi? I'm really tired," she cried out, her fatigue evident.

I placed my fingers in her hair, soothing her as my mind wandered back to Babli's story.

"I agree with you, beta," Bauji finally said during my next visit, his expression reflecting fatigue and sadness, likely from sleepless nights.

"Everything will be alright, Bauji. Please trust me," I assured him.

"I know, but I won't maintain any relation with her after the marriage," he declared.

"That is your decision, Bauji. I won't pressure you," I replied.

"Then call his parents today in your presence and talk to them," he said, his heart heavy.

Manoj's parents arrived an hour later, their faces displaying sadness, but they were willing to make sacrifices for their children.

"If both of you agree, we can have the wedding as soon as this month," I proposed.

Everyone in the room looked at me.

"What can we do, Vinodji, when our children have already made their decision? We'll fulfil our parental duties," they said.

Bauji appeared calm but deeply troubled inside, I knew.

"So, what do you think, Bauji?" I asked, the weight of the moment palpable.

"Ok beta, when everybody has accepted, whatever is decided will be agreeable to me also," he said with a sense of resignation.

"We will decide about it after talking to the Panditji and fix a date," Manoj's father continued, breaking the silence that had settled in the room, and with that, the meeting was disbanded.

As I sat there, a sense of satisfaction washed over me, though uncertainty still lingered like a shadow in the corner of my mind. Little did I know what lay in store for us.

But destiny is a fickle thing. Just 2 days later, Manoj's father dropped a bombshell. "Manoj is not ready for this relation," he confessed, a stark contradiction to his stance just days before.

Bauji, my father, exhaled a sigh of relief, grateful for the sudden twist of fate. He instructed Manoj's father to go back and deliver the message to Manoj himself: that he was not welcome in our house anymore.

My thoughts were jolted back to the present by Laxmi's soft voice. She requested water, and I obliged, trying to ease her discomfort. Her inquiry about our arrival time prompted me to ask the driver. "About an hour or so, we will reach sahib," he replied.

With the landscape passing by outside the window, my mind drifted back to the past and the turmoil of emotions that had gripped me then. I had been the mediator, orchestrating events in those critical moments, and Manoj's sudden denial had been both embarrassing and confounding. I was eager to meet with him to uncover the truth behind his change of heart.

The following day, I asked Ravi to summon Manoj to his doorstep. Manoj arrived with his father in tow. "I want to talk to Manoj for some time," I requested of his father.

"Vinod Ji, when everything is finished and he is denying, what will you talk to him about?" his father retorted.

Undeterred, I confronted Manoj directly, asking, "Manoj, why are you denying now?" His silence spoke volumes, leaving me feeling helpless and defeated.

I reluctantly accepted that the matter had been concluded, and I instructed Babli not to engage with Manoj any longer.

Time flowed inexorably onward, and life carried on. Then, one fine day, a knock on the door sent shockwaves through me. "What happened now?" I inquired sarcastically, unable to hide my surprise.

"Please, let me in first," Manoj pleaded, standing with folded hands.

"I was frightened of my father at that time, but I couldn't bear to be without Babli. I still want to marry her," he confessed.

I was torn, remembering the arduous journey of convincing Bauji, only for Manoj to backtrack, allowing him to breathe a sigh of relief. I couldn't bear to disturb him again on this matter.

"I am not in a position to narrate the things once again to Bauji, and you should also forget it," I firmly told him. His tears mirrored the despair of a child who had lost a cherished toy, and his pleas for help tugged at my heartstrings.

Finally, he proposed a daring idea: "What if we go away and get married as adults?" I was left stunned, urging him to give me some time to contemplate his proposition.

Laxmi's voice once again brought me back to the present, where she was growing increasingly uncomfortable. I did my best to comfort her, offering her a shoulder to lean on.

"We will reach soon. I know it's not easy, but we must be patient," I reassured her, feeling my own restlessness grow as I watched her tears fall.

As the journey continued, I closed my eyes and delved once more into the tumultuous story of Babli, Manoj, and the choices that had torn their lives apart.

I turned to Laxmi after Manoj's departure, hoping for her insight. "No, no, it's not possible now. I am against it," she responded, mirroring my reservations.

"They may choose to elope and get married in a temple. What then?" I pressed, leaving her momentarily silent.

"Mummy, can you imagine what will happen if they go away and get married on their own?" Laxmi voiced her concerns to her mother the next day.

Her mother, astute and perceptive, weighed the consequences of saying no to them at this juncture. "You should consult Vinodji, see what he thinks," she suggested, although arriving at a decision was far from easy.

One fateful afternoon, I received a call from Ravi that sent shivers down my spine. "Jijaji, please come immediately, Babli has been missing for 7-8 hours," he urgently pleaded.

"I'll be there as soon as I can," I assured him, recognising the gravity of the situation.

Upon arriving at Babli's house, we discovered a letter hidden in her cupboard, revealing her intentions to marry Manoj. Laxmi's mother shared the news, and we promptly visited Manoj's home to inquire about his whereabouts.

Manoj's father emerged from the house, and we presented the letter as evidence. "Please help us find both of them, or we will take legal action against Manoj," we implored.

But Manoj's father issued a stern warning, threatening us with dire consequences if we involved the police. The heated argument that ensued was futile, devoid of meaning or substance.

Defeated but determined, we decided to report the matter to the police. They swiftly arrested Manoj's father and vowed to keep him in custody until both Babli and Manoj were located. The ensuing drama sent ripples through the community, leaving everyone with unanswered questions.

Laxmi's mother and father were subjected to threats and taunts by Manoj's family and relatives whenever they stepped outside. Matters escalated to the point where they were forced to abandon their home and seek refuge in Yamuna Vihar, where one of my sisters resided. They had no choice but to sell their house, a painful and humiliating turn of events.

As I was jolted back to the present, Laxmi's voice reached my ears once more. "May I sit down?" she asked.

"Of course, please, take a seat," I replied, my mind still haunted by the memories of a tumultuous past that had reshaped our lives in unimaginable ways.

"How are you feeling now?" I whispered; my voice filled with concern.

Her response was a mere murmur, "A little better."

The journey had been arduous, and the destination seemed elusive. Laxmi had drifted into a fitful sleep, leaving me alone with the ghosts of our shared history. Lost in the labyrinth of memories, I barely noticed when Babli, our faithful companion, broke the silence.

"Would you like to eat or drink something?" Babli inquired; her voice laced with compassion.

Laxmi's answer came softly, "No, no, I will not take anything."

"Then please try to take rest," Babli urged, her eyes reflecting our mutual exhaustion. "We are about to reach the destination."

"Okay," Laxmi conceded, her voice tinged with weariness. "There is no other option except to wait."

As we continued our journey, I clung to the hope that the hospital would be our salvation. My thoughts wandered back to Babli's tumultuous past, a story filled with trials and tribulations.

A week later, a call disrupted the quietude of our lives. It was Manoj, Laxmi's brother.

"Jijaji, Namaste," he greeted.

"Namaste, Manoj," I replied, curiosity piqued. "Where are you? Everybody is looking for you."

"We wanted to meet," he confessed.

My words faltered, overwhelmed by the events that had unfolded since our last encounter. Turning to Laxmi, I broached the subject of their reunion.

"I think we should," she agreed, though her countenance remained shrouded in sorrow.

And so, we embarked on a journey to meet the newlyweds, but there was no joy in our hearts. Instead, a shadow of melancholy hung over us, casting a pall on the occasion. When we finally met them, they touched our feet, their faces etched with fear.

"Didi, is anything wrong at our homes?" they asked, their voices trembling.

Laxmi, tears welling in her eyes, revealed the heartbreaking truth. "Everything is ruined there."

Their destiny had played a cruel hand, and they were left adrift in the world, burdened by their tender age. Even our own parents were reluctant to embrace them, citing the actions of their families as justification.

Time passed, and life meandered on its unpredictable course. Then, one day, Manoj resurfaced in our lives.

"Jijaji, this is Manoj," he announced.

Surprised by his sudden reappearance, I inquired, "Oh, from where are you calling? Is everything fine now? How is Babli?"

"I am residing in a rented house now in Pandav Nagar," Manoj replied, his tone carrying a sense of urgency. "Please come to our home."

With reluctance, we ventured to their new abode. Little did we know that this visit would shatter our expectations. As we waited inside, Manoj abruptly left, leaving us bewildered.

After a prolonged silence, he returned with his grandmother, whose words were laden with accusation and anger.

"Please, Dadiji, you don't know the whole story," I implored, attempting to defuse the situation.

"You are misbehaving with my dadiji, Jijaji," Manoj interjected, defending his grandmother.

The tension in the room escalated as accusations flew. It became apparent that we had been brought here not for reconciliation, but to endure an unprovoked insult.

"You may get out and never come to our house from now onwards," Manoj thundered, his words laced with bitterness. "You insulted my dadiji. Also, take Babli along."

At that moment, Shalu, a small child of around 2 or 3 years old, rested in our laps, a symbol of innocence amidst the turmoil. It was a deeply humiliating experience, one that left us scarred and speechless.

Vowing never to cross paths with Manoj again, I shielded myself from further emotional turmoil. Destiny, it seemed, revelled in playing its inscrutable games.

Lost in my thoughts, I was abruptly brought back to the present by Babli's voice.

"Jijaji," she called repeatedly, pulling me from my reverie. "Ah, what happened?" I asked, disoriented.

"Please ask the driver how much time it will take," she pleaded.

With a heavy heart, I inquired about our progress from the driver, who delivered disheartening news.

"There is a lot of rush on the way, and it will take more than one hour now."

Turning my attention to Laxmi, I asked softly, "How are you feeling now?"

"A little better," she replied, her eyes reflecting the pain she tried to conceal. I had known her for over 3 decades, and I could sense her suffering. My gaze then drifted to Babli, who had transformed in countless ways since our first encounter in that rented house. Manoj had become a successful interior decorator, and life had taken unexpected turns.

My thoughts once again wandered to the story of Babli and Manoj. 3 years had passed, and the bitterness of our previous encounter had faded into distant memory.

"Laxmi, I met Babli and Manoj last Tuesday!" Laxmi's mother exclaimed excitedly over the phone.

Laxmi, incredulous, questioned, "How, mummy? How did you meet them?"

Laxmi's mother shared the story of her chance encounter with Babli and Manoj at the Hanuman Mandir in Yamuna Bazar.

"How are they doing now?" Laxmi inquired eagerly.

"They were doing well in life," her mother assured her.

With a newfound curiosity and a desire for closure, Laxmi insisted that we meet them again.

"No, it is not possible now," I hesitated, my apprehensions resurfacing.

Reluctantly, I agreed, "Okay, we will go, but I don't want to meet them after that."

As the days passed, the moment of reunion arrived. At the Hanuman Mandir, when we finally laid eyes on them, Laxmi's excitement was palpable.

"Here they are!" she cheered; her joy infectious.

Overwhelmed by emotions, I couldn't help but reach out to Manoj. "Manoj, please come. Don't touch my feet, but just hug me tight," I implored, surprising even myself.

In that poignant moment, I let go of the past, embracing him as if nothing had ever transpired. It was a reflection of my nature; I may harbour anger, but when someone takes the first step, I am quick to forgive.

Laxmi, too, embraced Babli, and tears flowed freely. The bitterness of the past dissipated, replaced by a shared sense of relief and reconciliation.

"How are you both doing now? Where do you reside? Have your parents forgiven you?" We exchanged stories and caught up, grateful to find that they had found their footing in life. Though Manoj's family had accepted their relationship, the wounds from the past still festered, a stark reminder of the tumultuous journey they had endured.

As time flowed on, Babli and Manoj's lives took on new dimensions. And amidst it all, they were blessed with a boy and a girl, a testament to their resilience in the face of adversity.

When I first met Manoj, we were young, naive souls back then, as we crossed paths in the intricate tapestry of life. Over the years, our lives took unexpected twists and turns, but our connection grew stronger with each passing day. Today, I can boldly declare that he is more than just a friend; he's a brother in every sense of the word. For true brotherhood is not confined to shared blood, but rather, it blooms from the nurturing bonds that time and experiences create. While anyone can be a sibling by birth, it takes a heart brimming with character and kindness to be a loving brother to one's in-laws.

The relentless march of time swept us forward, and blessings rained upon us. Babli, our beloved, was gifted with a son and a daughter. The children were a source of unending joy, and their visits to our abode were always met with Shalu and Vicky playfully bickering over who would cradle the adorable baby girl.

"Papa, didi won't let me hold Guddu. Please tell her!" Vicky complained, his young face etched with frustration.

"Shalu, be kind and let him hold her; he's just a little boy," I urged, my voice a calm river of reason.

"You always take his side, papa. I won't talk to you anymore," Shalu retorted, her small frame brimming with righteous indignation.

When I eventually coaxed her to my side, placing Guddu in her arms, all resentments melted away in the sheer ecstasy of holding the precious baby.

Children, with their pure hearts, seldom hold onto anger for long, unlike us, complex adults.

Tragedy cast its shadow upon us when Babli's father fell gravely ill. The doctors delivered a grim verdict - there was no hope for his recovery. "Call your relatives to bid him farewell," the doctor advised.

I turned to Bauji, seeking his wishes. "Would you like to meet Babli and Manoj?" I inquired.

"No, no, I don't want to," he replied, his voice heavy with sorrow.

"Bauji, seeing your children happy and thriving will bring you solace," I gently persuaded him.

"Okay, beta, as you wish," he relented.

In my determination to reunite them, I reached out to Mukesh, my cousin and Laxmi's youngest sister's husband. He was entwined with our family in more ways than one.

"Namaste, Mukesh, how are you?" I greeted him, hoping for his assistance.

"Tell me what you need, Vinod. I'd do anything for you," he assured.

"Can you go to Manoj's home and ask him to meet Bauji secretly? The doctor believes his time is short," I implored.

"But how can I go there?" Mukesh hesitated.

"No one will recognise you in their home, that's why I'm sending you," I explained, sealing their reunion.

Tears flowed freely when they finally met. A few days later, Bauji's time had come, but I found solace in reuniting them one last time.

Mukesh was bound to me in 2 distinct ways. He was my maternal cousin through a complex web of familial ties, and he had also become my brother-in-law when Baby, Laxmi's youngest sister, married him.

But fate had other plans for us, initially opposing Baby and Mukesh's union. My objections, rooted in my respect for my Tauji's wishes, led to tensions within the family.

However, following Tauji's passing, my mother longed to renew relations with Mukesh's family, even desiring to tie a rakhi to Mukesh's father. Her wish was initially thwarted by my father and me, as we held close to Tauji's memory. But eventually, my mother established a relationship with them.

Two years passed, and the topic of Baby and Mukesh's marriage resurfaced.

"Vinodji, can we discuss Baby's matrimonial alliance with Mukesh's family?" Laxmi's mother inquired one day.

I hesitated; my objections grounded in my reluctance to accept that family. However, in the end, I conceded to their wishes, recognising the importance of maintaining these familial bonds.

After their marriage, Baby faced hardships in Mukesh's family, as I had anticipated. The environment was far from ideal, but 2 daughters and a son were born into their household. Arguments over Mukesh's alleged extramarital affair stirred in the neighbourhood, casting a dark cloud over their lives. To make matters worse, Baby fell ill, eventually diagnosed with diabetes and depression, a cruel turn of fate for such a young soul.

One day, Mukesh called us with a desperate plea. "Didi, please come immediately. Baby is seriously ill," he implored.

We rushed to their home, joined by Ravi, Poonam, and Titu. However, the situation took a devastating turn, as the doctor declared Baby dead. Chaos reigned in the wake of this sudden tragedy, and while many urged us to involve the police, we refrained, mindful of the young children left behind.

My wandering thoughts were interrupted by Babli's voice.

"Jijaji, your phone is ringing," she called out, and I snapped back to the present.

"Papa, how is mummy feeling now?" Shalu's voice emanated from the other end.

"She's in pain, Shalu," I replied, my voice trembling.

"Have patience, papa. She'll be alright. God is great. Please take care of her. Should I come in the ambulance to help?" Shalu offered.

"No, no. Babli and I are here. You just relax," I assured her.

As I handed Babli some water, I couldn't help but reflect on the twists and turns of destiny that had brought us to this moment. If my mother had not persevered in her efforts to maintain relations with Mukesh's family, Baby and Mukesh might never have met. Our reluctance had been no match for fate's design.

And then, my thoughts shifted to my own journey with Laxmi.

"Listen, I'm not feeling well," Laxmi confessed one night while we lay in bed, her pregnancy casting a shadow of concern over her. I sprang into action, determined to protect the woman I loved.

"What happened? Shall I call Mataji?" I asked, concern evident in my voice.

"Yes, please call her. I am feeling a lot of pain," she replied, her voice trembling with discomfort.

"Mataji, please come up immediately. Laxmi is not feeling well," I called, my voice quivering.

"Please call an auto immediately to go to the hospital," Mataji urged as she reached our room.

"Please come slowly," I reassured Laxmi, my hands trembling as I arranged for an auto.

The time on the clock read 11 at night, and the city's streets outside seemed desolate at that hour.

"Please don't worry; we will reach the hospital soon," I said, trying to comfort Laxmi.

"Okay, but there is a lot of pain," she replied, her voice strained.

Racing through the quiet, deserted streets, we reached the hospital, which was a mere 5 minutes away from our home. With great trepidation, I admitted Laxmi to the labour room, my heart heavy with concern.

"Oh God, please take care of her," I prayed repeatedly, my thoughts consumed by worry. We spent the entire night at the hospital, anxiety and anticipation gnawing at our hearts. With no means to contact our relatives due to the absence of phones, we waited anxiously.

Finally, around 8 AM, the nurse called my name, breaking the long, tense silence.

"Yes, sister?" I asked, rushing to her side.

"Come inside," she beckoned, her face unreadable.

"Is everything alright?" I inquired, my heart pounding in my chest.

In response, she placed a precious bundle in my lap. "See this child," she urged. "Can you tell if it's a boy or a girl?"

"This is a girl," I announced with a smile.

"Congratulations. She's quite fragile, and we'll need to keep her in the nursery," the nurse informed me.

"How is Laxmi?" I inquired anxiously.

"She's also fine, but you'll be able to see her in 2 hours," the nurse replied.

"Congratulations, Mataji, a baby girl has come to our home," I exclaimed, my voice quivering with excitement. It was our first child, and the emotions were overwhelming.

Mataji, however, seemed lost in her thoughts, and her reaction was subdued. "What happened? You didn't react," I probed.

"Nothing, another girl child," she whispered softly, tears welling up in her eyes.

"Come on, Mataji, girl or boy, it doesn't matter," I consoled her, enfolding her in a warm embrace and wiping away her tears.

"I will throw a party, boy or girl, this is my first child," I declared. Mataji remained silent.

I celebrated the birth of our daughter with great enthusiasm when we returned home, and our relatives joined in the festivities. Over the years, Shalu became the heart and soul of our family, a caring and loving presence.

In my family, I had 6 sisters and one brother. My brother had 4 daughters and one son. When Shalu was born, my mother was deeply disappointed and wept. I reassured her that I was overjoyed, but it took her some time to accept it. Nonetheless, I hosted a grand party because I was elated to have a little angel in our home. As the years passed, Shalu grew closer to her grandmother.

"Papa, I'll turn 18 this year. Let's celebrate my 18th birthday with a grand party and invite all our relatives," Shalu suggested one day.

Time passed swiftly, and in March 1997, Shalu was on the cusp of adulthood. "Yes, Shalu, we will definitely celebrate your 18th birthday in grand style," I promised. We were determined to grant her every wish and desire in life, but fate had other plans.

"Listen, Mataji isn't eating properly," Laxmi informed me one day, concern etched on her face.

"What happened, Mataji? Are you not feeling well? You're not eating properly," I inquired.

"Nothing, there's some pain and heaviness in my abdomen," she replied.

"Okay, tomorrow we'll go to the doctor," I reassured her.

The following day, after a thorough examination, the doctor suggested an ultrasound.

I consulted my cousin, who had connections at AIIMS, for a prompt appointment. "Please come tomorrow morning," he said.

"Shall we go for a biopsy as well?" the doctor inquired.

"Sure, please do what's best for her," I replied.

"Okay, we'll have the report by tomorrow."

The next day, my cousin called with news that shook my world. "Please listen carefully, Vinod."

"What happened? Have the reports come?" I asked, my voice quivering.

"Abdominal cancer has been detected," he informed me.

I was rendered speechless. "Hello, are you listening?"

"Yes, I'm sorry, is that correct?" I asked, seeking confirmation.

"Yes, please come with me to AIIMS tomorrow. We'll consult a senior doctor," he said.

The news was a gut-wrenching blow that I couldn't bring myself to share with anyone except Laxmi. She, too, was in shock. I had lost my father 6 years earlier, but with Mataji by our side, I had still felt blessed. Now, a grim cloud hung over our family.

"What did Amba inform?" Mataji asked, her eyes searching our faces. "You look very tense; is everything alright?"

"Yes, Mataji, the reports are fine, and there's a stone in your abdomen. Please come with us to the hospital tomorrow. A senior doctor will examine you," I said, concealing the grim reality.

"Okay, I will come," she agreed.

The following day, we visited the AIIMS senior doctor at his clinic where he examined Mataji and delivered the crushing verdict. "Bahanji, you'll be alright," he said, comforting her as she sat outside. He then called me inside.

"I've conducted a thorough examination. She has terminal-stage cancer. There's nothing more we can do, and she has less than 6 months to live," he revealed.

I fell into a contemplative silence, mulling over the grave prognosis. The doctor's words hung heavy in the air, a pall of uncertainty settling over us.

"I can tell you how to take care of her now," he offered, breaking the silence. "Please take her to Safdarjung Hospital tomorrow. You will have to make efforts to get her registered in the hospital. They will start radiotherapy and then chemotherapy. She will feel less pain, but her life will not be improved."

I couldn't help but inquire about the doctor's fee. "What's your fee, doctor?" I asked, my voice trembling with a mix of gratitude and desperation.

The doctor's response was unexpected, "Nothing. I have not done anything," he humbly stated.

"Please, doctor, take your fee at least," I insisted, knowing that the medical profession deserved its due.

"Okay, please pay Rs. 200/- as a token amount," he acquiesced.

"What a kind-hearted doctor, Manoj!" I remarked, impressed by his generosity.

"Yes, he is," my companion agreed, his voice heavy with the gravity of the situation.

Silence hung in the room as we grappled with the dire diagnosis. We had yet to share the grim news with Shalu, our beloved daughter, who was particularly close to her grandmother. She had been insisting on a grand birthday celebration, her innocence shining through amidst the shadows of our despair. It was a heart-wrenching dilemma we faced.

In the following months, we dutifully followed the doctor's instructions, witnessing our beloved matriarch's valiant struggle against a relentless adversary. It was a gruelling five-month ordeal, and when she finally passed away, Shalu was inconsolable. The loss of her grandmother had shattered her world, and the pain was too much for her tender heart to bear.

Years passed, and Shalu completed her graduation. Friends and relatives began to nudge me toward the idea of finding her a suitable match, but I resisted. Shalu was focused on her studies, and I believed that everything was in the hands of the Almighty. When the time was right, we would fulfil our duties.

One morning, a call from my niece Anju brought unexpected news. She had learned of a young man in our neighbourhood, well-educated and working in a reputable company. He was set to leave for Bombay on a posting, and an opportunity to meet him had arisen.

"Let's see," I replied to Anju's suggestion, trying to maintain my stance of not hurrying Shalu into marriage.

My wife, Laxmi, overheard our conversation and added her perspective. "But if we don't explore such opportunities, no one will tell us anything in the future."

Reluctantly, I agreed to meet the young man and his family, making a cautious step toward considering Shalu's future. Our visit to their home was promising, with everything seemingly favourable.

When we returned from the meeting, Shalu confronted us, having been informed by her younger brother, Vicky, about our secret mission.

"I don't want to marry at such a young age, papa," she cried, tears welling up in her eyes. Her concern for her education was evident.

I reassured her, "Don't cry, we haven't made any decisions yet."

Shalu demanded an explanation, "But why did you go there in the first place?"

I explained, "It's a process, Shalu. We start by looking at potential matches, and then we decide. It takes time."

Her tears subsided, and she reluctantly agreed to consider the proposal because the boy's family was amiable, and Vicky had managed to convince her, despite his own youth. Moreover, the prospect of the boy's posting in Mumbai, a city where her idols, Sachin Tendulkar and Aamir Khan, resided, held a childlike appeal for her.

As time went on, we eagerly awaited a response from the young man's family, but none came. Frustration mounted as their excuses for the delay multiplied.

"Please give them a call," Laxmi urged, unwilling to accept the silence.

I hesitated, fearing the worst. "What's the use? They will inform us when the boy returns."

Time dragged on, and the silence gnawed at our hopes. I finally resolved not to make any more inquiries.

Then, one day, as we returned from a wedding ceremony, we were greeted by a sobbing Laxmi.

"What happened? Why are you crying?" I asked in alarm.

She managed to choke out the news between her tears, "There was a call from the boy's father. They are coming tomorrow."

Relief and excitement washed over me, and I thanked the heavens for answering my prayers.

The following day, the prospective groom's family came to our home. They requested to speak with Shalu privately after the initial formalities.

In the evening, their decision was revealed - they had agreed to the match. We celebrated the news with joy and agreed to a formal "roka" ceremony.

"Papa, I received a call from Deepak, the groom," Shalu approached me with a request.

"Alright, you may go, but come back early," I consented, exchanging knowing glances with my wife, Laxmi.

Shalu's visit with the groom before the wedding was unconventional for our time, and we anxiously awaited her return. Our relief upon her safe return was palpable, and we could finally enjoy a meal without the weight of uncertainty. The wedding preparations proceeded smoothly, and we found ourselves immersed in joy and celebration, grateful for the blessings we had received from above.

In the quiet corridors of destiny, our son-in-law, a genius wrapped in understanding, emerged as a guiding light. A beacon that shone not only through the grace of God but also with the blessings bestowed upon us by our parents. Manoj, with his unwavering commitment, bore the weight of responsibilities—physical, mental, and financial—allowing us to forge ahead, the ceremony marked with joyous celebrations.

Yet, destiny, that mysterious weaver of fates, wove its own threads into our tapestry. Strings of attachment veiled even our happiest moments. As if on cue, the present collided with the plaintive cry of Laxmi, piercing the narrative of bliss.

"Ah, ah," she sobbed, caught in the throes of pain. Concern etched across my face, I implored, "What happened? Babli, fetch some water for her." Laxmi writhed, and I reassured her, "Be patient; we are almost there."

The echoes of Shalu's wedding lingered in my thoughts. Post the ceremonial bidai and the ritualistic pag phera, as relaxation settled in, Laxmi confessed to feeling unwell. I dismissed it as the exhaustion of matrimony, only to summon a doctor when her condition worsened.

"How Is she, doctor?" I inquired anxiously after the examination.

"I administered an injection. Nothing serious. Just give her some rest," the doctor assured.

After 4 hours of restless slumber, Laxmi awoke with weakened faculties. A subsequent visit to the doctor unveiled the harsh reality – a clot in her brain, a consequence of soaring blood pressure. A paralytic attack mandated a protracted recovery, casting a pall of gloom upon us. Our household, in disarray from the recent nuptials, was juxtaposed against Laxmi's hospitalisation. It marked the first occasion I cried out to God, a desperate plea for her swift recovery.

After 6 agonising days, Laxmi emerged from the hospital, bedridden and facing a six-month recovery period. Vicky and I, clueless about domestic affairs, grappled with the question of care. Manoj, once again, stepped in with a generous offer.

"Don't worry, Sharmaji. We'll take her to our home. When she can walk, she can return to yours," he reassured.

In an act of selflessness, Manoj shouldered the responsibility, despite his parents' lingering displeasure. Laxmi spent over a month in their care before returning, leaving an indelible mark of gratitude in our hearts.

"Let's arrange for a physiotherapist to come home," I suggested to Laxmi, breaking the silence.

"Okay, as you say," came her reply. The next day marked the commencement of physiotherapy sessions.

"Can we stop the physiotherapy from tomorrow?" Laxmi queried one day.

"Are you out of your mind? How will you recover fast then?" I questioned.

"I'm letting go of the maid too and will manage household chores myself," she declared.

I was taken aback. The financial strain post-marriage, hospital expenses, and ongoing medical costs left us in a dire crisis. Laxmi's resilience, however, proved crucial. She opted for self-sufficiency, turning daily chores into therapeutic exercises, speeding up her recovery.

"Ah, I want to vomit. Please help me sit!" Laxmi's plea snapped me back to the present. Hastily assisting her, I peered outside. Delhi loomed, yet a maddening traffic snarl thwarted our progress. It was 10 pm, and the realisation struck hours had slipped away, leaving my wife in anguish.

My thoughts again took me back to the past. In the corridors of reminiscence, the shadow of debt loomed large. Vicky's education, Laxmi's recovery, and my role as the sole breadwinner necessitated tough choices.

"Should we sell the flat?" I proposed to Laxmi one day.

"Impossible! What will society say? We can't sell our flat so soon after marriage," she fretted.

"Or should I take VRS?" I suggested.

"Are you mad? What will you do then?" She grew anxious.

The dilemma lingered, but a glimmer of hope emerged. I broached the idea of altered office hours with my part-time employer, hoping to supplement income through loans and EMIs.

"I'll consider it," the CMD replied, setting the stage for a challenging juggling act between work, sleep, and financial recovery.

In the dark alleys of exploitation, I choose silence over retaliation. A month later, a breakthrough—3 AM, a conversation with the CMD. The proposal to alter my hours was on the table.

"What were you talking about, VK?" he queried.

"Sir, I can come at 3 PM daily if you need my services," I replied, embracing the chance for a brighter future.

"OK, what are you expecting?" he inquired, his gaze unwavering.

"Sir, it will be a full-time job then. You take this into consideration," I replied, the weight of impending decisions hanging in the air.

"OK, I will give you Rs.XXX," he declared, a meagre offering that I reluctantly accepted. In the grand scheme of things, it was a pittance, but in the turmoil of our financial struggles, it felt like a merciful intervention from a higher power.

The relief, however, came at a steep cost. Eighteen-hour workdays, a relentless grind that gnawed at my health and well-being. In the silent hours of the night, Laxmi, my wife, bore the solitude of our home, oscillating between day and night duties in my relentless pursuit of financial stability.

"Jijaji, where have we reached now?" Babli's voice cut through my thoughts, pulling me back to the present.

"We are quite near now. I think it will not take more than half an hour if there is no jam on the way," I reassured her, glancing at the urban landscape beyond the car window.

"Oh God, didi is getting restless now," Babli fretted.

"Please have patience," I implored Laxmi. Her silence spoke volumes, a symphony of restlessness and helplessness that mirrored my own sense of powerlessness.

Amidst the journey's turbulence, my mind wandered to our 25th Anniversary. The idea of celebration surfaced an attempt to infuse joy into our strained lives. But Laxmi, practical and resolute, resisted the notion.

"Shall we call some relatives at home? We will bring some food items from outside and celebrate our anniversary in some sense," I suggested.

"No, please don't. On one hand, we are in deep debt, and on the other, we are throwing a party," Laxmi replied, her gaze fixed on the reality we couldn't escape.

"It will not be so costly, dear," I insisted, yearning for a moment of respite.

"No, we can't do it. We will do it some other time," she asserted, unmoved by my plea.

Our 25th anniversary unfolded quietly, a corner of the room hosting a simple meal of dal and roti. Together, we found solace in each other, a celebration of togetherness in the face of adversity.

As time progressed, the weight of Laxmi's illness compounded. The routine neuro checks unveiled a new challenge – a tablet for depression. Shocked and concerned, I confronted the doctor, questioning the prescription.

"Why didn't you tell me earlier?" I asked Laxmi, the revelation unsettling.

"I was anxious that you will leave everything. Sometimes, I am afraid at night when alone," she confided.

"You should have told me," I reproached.

"What would you have done?" she asked.

"I would have left the job. I don't want anything else except the well-being of my family members," I declared, torn between professional obligations and familial responsibilities.

A cloud of uncertainty loomed as I contemplated taking Voluntary Retirement. The burden of debt had lifted, but the decision to depart from my career path would bring new challenges. Consulting our children became imperative.

"Shalu, shall I go ahead with taking VRS?" I asked, laying bare the dilemma.

"What happened, papa? Why this question all of a sudden?" Shalu inquired, caught off guard.

"Your mother is getting anxious at night when alone. The doctor prescribed her medicine for depression," I explained, the gravity of the situation unfolding.

"What!!!" Shalu exclaimed, grappling with the unforeseen revelation.

"Mummy is not comfortable with my working hours, and I have to be with her. There is no other option but to take VRS," I elucidated, seeking understanding.

"What will you do then?" she questioned.

"I am working part-time. All loans have come to an end now," I reassured her.

"But it's not enough!" she protested.

"I will do something else also," I asserted, facing the uncertainty with determination.

A pivotal conversation with the HR head marked the finality of my decision. "I want to take VRS," I declared, unravelling the threads of my professional life.

"What are you talking about, Mr. Sharma? It's the peak of your career, and you are making this decision. What's the problem?" the HR head responded, baffled by the abrupt choice.

Letting the truth spill, I explained, "Continuous night duty, my wife alone at night, depressed. Her well-being is my priority, not my career."

The HR head, understanding the weight of my sentiments, proposed an alternative – changing office timings. However, anticipating future demands, I declined, my resolution unwavering.

Amidst the ebb and flow of life's uncertainties, a pivotal moment beckoned—a choice that would reshape the trajectory of my existence. After persistent entreaties, the management, begrudgingly, acquiesced to my request for relief, albeit with the stipulation to linger a while longer until further arrangements were made.

The departure from Indian Express, my professional sanctuary for 15 years, left an unmistakable void in the tapestry of my life. Amid the ensuing emptiness, the CMD of the part-time office, a discerning figure, broached the subject of my recent Voluntary Retirement.

"I understand you took VRS from Indian Express?" the CMD inquired one day, his discerning eyes probing.

"Yes, sir. How do you know?" I responded, a tinge of surprise colouring my words.

"Leave it. Please accept our offer for a full-time job in our company on whatever amount you deem fit," he proposed, extending an olive branch in the form of employment.

"Let me think. I can't make a decision in haste. There is still a hangover from the media job. Let me take some rest first," I replied, my reluctance apparent.

The offer, laden with implications, held no allure. The CMD's demeanour with his employees had left a sour taste, particularly in the realm of full-time employment where dependence on him was inevitable. Contemplation ensued.

An alternative beckoned in the form of a job offer at Atlas Cycles, an opportunity I embraced. The CMD, however, persisted, urging me to continue my part-time role in the evenings even if the prospect of a full-time position was declined.

Destiny, that elusive force weaving the threads of our lives, was a concept I grappled with as the circumstances unfolded. The logical result of actions taken, the intersection of circumstances, and the influence of those around us—destiny was a force that demanded acknowledgement. In the whispers of life's grand design, a call from a higher power reverberated, urging a surrender to the inexorable flow of events.

My son Vicky's voice, emerging from the present, anchored me back to the reality of the ambulance journey.

"Papa, how is mummy now? I am coming to the ambulance," Vicky's voice resonated from the other car.

"No, she is alright, and we are about to reach now," I assured him, my voice a steady reassurance.

In the embrace of familial concern, my mind meandered to a time when Vicky's entry into our lives brought unparalleled joy. The nurse's announcement, "Congratulations! You are blessed with a baby boy," echoed through the hospital corridors. Mataji, overcome with emotion, shed tears of joy, grateful for the newfound addition to our family.

Yet, life's capricious nature unveiled its darker shades when Vicky, in his infancy, faced a health crisis. Laxmi's observant eye detected an anomaly, and a visit to the doctor ensued.

"See, the mouth of Vicky is being turned towards the left," Laxmi voiced her concern.

"He is a child, and making such things is the habit of children," I dismissed, the weight of worry not yet apparent.

"Sometimes, please be serious, see his face carefully," Laxmi persisted.

A visit to the doctor revealed unsettling news—Vicky required hospitalisation for observation. Shocked and disheartened, we faced the uncertainty of his condition.

"We have to give him electric shocks," the doctor declared, his words plunging us into despair.

Amidst the anguished cries of our small boy, helpless in the face of medical intervention, we grappled with the heart-wrenching decision. On the fourth day, unable to bear the torment any longer, I pleaded with the doctor to cease the shocks, placing the well-being of our child above all else.

"What happened to Vicky?" a concerned relative inquired during a visit to Yamuna Vihar.

"Doctors say it's facial paralysis. I don't know what to do. I am tired now," I confessed, wearied by the relentless trial's life had thrown our way.

"Have faith, Vinod. There is a person in Hatheen near Palwal who cures such diseases, and a lot of people have been benefited. He resides in a small temple," my sister's sister-in-law suggested, offering a glimmer of hope.

"If somebody suggests such a thing at the first place, I would have rejected the proposal instantly, but at this stage, when doctors are not sure about the cure, there was no other option but to go there and start treatment," I reflected, acknowledging the twist of fate that led us to uncharted realms.

"Please bring some material from the grocery shop," the Baba in the temple requested during our visit, his words imbued with an air of mystique.

"OK, Baba, but he will be alright, na?" I asked hopefully.

"Please have faith in God. He is giving grief and relief both, and at what time, only He decides," Baba's words lingered, a mantra of hope in the face of life's tumultuous currents.

"Okay, Baba," I uttered, surrendering to the mystique surrounding the sage-like figure before us. His instructions, a whispered promise of remedy, were delivered to Laxmi after he meticulously concocted the prescribed medicine.

"I am sure after taking one pouch with goat milk, he will be alright. However, he is a very small child, and taking such bitter medicine in one go is not possible for him. Please give one pouch 2-3 times to him. He may spit, but please just help him to gallop the whole medicine. After that, please cover him with a blanket for at least one hour. Please bring him after 15 days to me," Baba articulated, his voice carrying the weight of certainty.

Yet, it was August, and the stifling humidity clung to our bodies like an oppressive shroud. Blanketing a child, much less in such weather, seemed an insurmountable challenge.

"We will try, Babaji," we assured, the words leaving our lips with a hopeful undertone.

"God bless you. I hope when you come next time to me, he will be alright," Baba offered a glimmer of optimism, a beacon in the uncertain journey that lay ahead.

The assurance bestowed upon us by Baba surpassed the guarantees of qualified medical professionals. Grateful for this ray of hope, I silently thanked the divine forces and fervently prayed for the swift recovery of my ailing child.

"Thu thu," echoed through the room as we attempted to administer the medicine to Vicky. The bitter concoction prompted resistance, and with considerable effort, we managed to coax him into ingesting it.

Within a week, signs of recovery manifested on Vicky's face, a testament to the efficacy of Baba's remedy. The satisfaction that accompanied this improvement was profound, the assurance that we had finally arrived at the right destination.

"Quite good. He is almost 75% cured," Baba pronounced during our subsequent visit after 15 days.

"Yes, Baba, we are thankful to you," we expressed our gratitude, the weight of worry lifted from our shoulders.

Once again, he prescribed the same medicine, assuring us that there would be no need to return, as Vicky would now be on the path to complete recovery. The caveat: continue administering the medicine for the next 3 months.

Thrilled by these words, we extended our gratitude not only to Baba but also to the serendipitous guide who had led us to this saviour. Vicky, in due time, fully recovered. A year later, faced with a recurrence, we promptly sought Baba's intervention and bid farewell to the ailment once and for all.

Vicky, the embodiment of love and care, navigated the challenges of life with maturity that belied his years. In the tumultuous transition of Shalu's marriage during his 11th standard, Vicky displayed a deep understanding of the family's financial struggles and his mother's illness. His selflessness extended to forgoing tuition, a luxury he needed but chose to relinquish.

The pursuit of academic aspirations, however, unfurled an unforeseen challenge. Vicky's dreams of pursuing B. Tech faced a setback when the entrance exam results did not align with his aspirations.

"Sorry, papa, my rank doesn't allow me to take admission in B. Tech in college. What should I do now? I want to do engineering. Only one result is awaited from Manipal University. I hope to get admission there," Vicky confided in me.

A letter from Manipal University brought jubilation, signalling an opportunity for a fresh start. However, the bustling chaos during the admission process unveiled a harsh reality.

"In which branch do you want to take admission?" the official inquired during Vicky's turn.

"Electronics and Communication," Vicky responded optimistically.

"Sorry, gentlemen, because of such a rush we are not able to give admission in such a branch. However, you can inform me of your second option," the official announced.

"Computer Science," Vicky declared, his hopes momentarily crushed.

"Okay, you are on the waiting list. We will inform you within a week, and you may go now," the official conveyed, leaving us with a sense of uncertainty.

The subsequent revelation that Vicky's preferred branch was unavailable compounded the disappointment. Yet, we returned home, determined to navigate this unexpected turn of events.

A glimmer of hope emerged when Vicky discovered an opportunity in Karnataka. With newfound optimism, we embarked on a journey, securing admission with a sense of relief. Vicky's resilience, coupled with his understanding of the family's financial constraints, shone through as he navigated the challenges of hostel life without placing additional burdens on us.

Amidst these triumphs, life's unpredictable twists continued. A phone call from Ravi, Laxmi's brother, brought news of Titu's accident.

"Jijaji, Titu met with an accident," Ravi's voice crackled through the phone, urgency tinged with concern.

"Where is he? I am coming. Please don't worry. Everything will be alright," I assured Ravi, my resolve unwavering.

The intricate dynamics of familial relationships unfolded in the aftermath of Babli's marriage, where I stood as the lone link connecting the fragmented ties. The rift between Titu and the family widened, the scars of the past haunting him. Even the ritual of Raksha Bandhan, intended to bridge the gap, became a catalyst for further discord.

Titu, burdened by the haunting memories, distanced himself from the familial bonds, severing connections with Laxmi, Babli, and Ravi.

The news shattered the airwaves as Ravi's tearful voice spilled through the phone, delivering the devastating message, "Jijaji Titu is no more!" Confusion gripped me as I sought to understand the abrupt tragedy.

"What happened? Was he critical or something?" I inquired, desperation edging my words.

"I don't know," Ravi's response held a weight of helplessness.

As we arrived at AIIMS, the sombre reality awaited us in the mortuary. Seeking answers, we approached the doctor, our shock echoing through each word.

"What happened, doctor? In what condition was he brought here?" The question hung in the air, laden with disbelief.

"He met with an accident with a truck and was dead when brought here," came the chilling response.

The weight of the revelation pressed upon us, an avalanche of questions flooding our minds. What would become of his family? His children, still in their infancy, had lost their mother just 2 years ago. The tragedy unfolded before us, a cruel twist of fate.

Alone at home, Laxmi and I grappled with the aftermath, our thoughts consumed by Titu. Despite the severed ties, he remained a presence in our hearts, a child lost to circumstances.

Titu, young during our marriage, had witnessed the turmoil that engulfed his family after Babli's union. I had advised him against severing ties, understanding that familial bonds could not be dictated. Yet, he chose a different path, unwilling to grasp the complexity of the situation.

Bauji, crippled after an accident, turned to me for help. His plea for assistance for Titu, a young man with no earning member in the family, tugged at my heart.

"Vinodji, can you please do something?" Bauji's appeal was a desperate plea.

"I will try," I assured him.

Approaching my workplace, I sought aid from Mr. Goel, the head of the company.

"Sir, one of my relatives is in need of service. Can you do something?" I implored.

"What's his qualification?" Mr. Goel inquired.

"He has done 10th," I responded.

"That's not enough. How can I keep him?" scepticism laced his words.

"Sir, he is in dire need of money. His father is handicapped, and there is nobody in his family to take care," I pleaded.

"Hmm," he pondered. "Please send him to me tomorrow; I will see."

Thus, Titu found employment, providing a lifeline to his struggling family. The burden on Bauji lifted, and gratitude flowed profusely.

Over time, working in the same office, Titu and I developed a camaraderie. Bonding over shared experiences, including those involving Babli, we grew closer. Encouraged by my acceptance of Babli and Manoj after our chance encounter at Hanuman Mandir, I counselled Titu to let go of the past.

"Titu, I am going to Baddi for office work. Will you accompany me?" I proposed.

"You will do your official work; what should I do there?" he hesitated.

"We will go to Shimla after the work is done. It will take an hour or so," I suggested.

"Hmm," he remained conflicted.

"Don't think so much; take a pair of clothes with you and come to our place. We will take the Himalayan Queen in the morning," I insisted.

"OK, I will come," he relented.

In Shimla, amid moments of revelry, I broached the sensitive subject with Titu.

"I want to talk to you about Babli," I ventured.

"Please don't spoil the mood, Jijaji," he deflected.

As we indulged in an evening drinking session, I sought to impart wisdom.

"Please rethink, Titu. I am your elder brother and won't advise you on things that are not good," I implored.

"I know, but you have not seen, you have not borne what me and my family did," he resisted.

"I understand, Titu, but it was in the past. Both of them are very happy together now," I reasoned.

"No, I won't," he remained unyielding.

"I would have been with you if our sister was not happy. But today, what can we do? We all are human beings and commit mistakes, and so has Babli," I attempted to break through.

The room fell into a profound silence.

Returning from Shimla, Titu withdrew from our lives. Slowly but surely, the fragile threads of our relationship unravelled, culminating in an unspoken farewell.

"Sir, you can come inside the mortuary and see the body!" the hospital staff prompted, jolting me back to the present.

"Ah," I snapped back to awareness, and we entered the solemn chamber.

Titu lay there, peaceful in eternal rest. Laxmi and Babli, inconsolable, faced the cruel acceptance of the divine decree.

"Jijaji, Shalu is calling you," Babli informed me, pulling me back into the present from the labyrinth of Titu's memories.

"Oh, what happened?" I asked.

"Why were you not picking up the phone? It was ringing for a long time," Shalu questioned.

"Sorry, beta, I was lost in thought," I replied.

"How much time will it take now?" she inquired.

"I think it is not much, but the traffic on the road is a speed breaker," I responded, diverting my attention to Shalu's daughter.

"Congratulations! You have become a grandfather." A call from Deepak Ji brought joy into our lives. "We have been blessed with a baby girl."

"Thank-you, beta, for giving us such happiness. We are coming there," I responded joyfully.

"How are Gudia and Shalu?" I asked.

"They both are fine, and you can meet them," Deepak Ji reassured.

Shalu's daughter, a mirror image of her mother, nestled in my arms, and I couldn't help but remark, "She is very cute."

"Yes, papa, take care. She is very small," Shalu cautioned.

"I am feeling at present what I felt the first time I took you in my lap," I confessed, my eyes betraying a hint of emotion.

"No, papa, it's a matter of celebration," Shalu rejoiced.

"Oh yes, we will definitely celebrate this occasion as soon as you come home," I declared with excitement.

"Hello Shalu! Congratulations today is the sixth day, and there must be a havan at your home," I called Shalu on the sixth day.

"Yes, papa, we all are very happy," she replied.

"Hold on, papa. I will ring you back," she said in a hurry.

Unaware of the impending turmoil, I awaited her call, assuming the delay was due to the festivity at her residence.

After 2 to 3 hours, I decided to reach out again.

"Shalu, what happened? Why were you crying?" I inquired.

"Papa, Gudia is not well. She became unconscious when you called me, and that's why I disconnected your phone," she revealed with worry etched across her voice.

"Where are you at present?" I asked.

"At Maharaja Agrasen hospital," she replied.

"I am coming. Please don't worry. God is great," I consoled her, bracing myself for the unpredictable twists that life continued to unfurl.

"What happened, beta? What did the doctor say about Gudia?" I inquired; my voice tinged with concern.

"She doesn't have one artery that supplies blood to the heart," Shalu's response fell like a heavy blow.

"What! How can that be possible? She's so small," I exclaimed, shock reverberating in my words.

"Yes, but it's true," Shalu affirmed.

We embarked on a quest for answers, seeking solace in the halls of AIIMS and consulting with the head of cardiology at Escorts. Yet, the verdict remained unchanged—a heartbreaking revelation. This, our first grandchild, Shalu's firstborn, confronted with a life-altering condition.

During a prior journey to Manipal with Vicky, I had encountered a doctor in Bangalore, a pioneer in operating on a Pakistani child with a similar arterial anomaly. Urged by hope, we reached out to this seasoned professional.

"Can you bring the child to me at the earliest?" the doctor implored after reviewing the reports.

"We will, doctor, but what is the prognosis? Will she be alright?" I sought assurance.

"I will be in a position to give an opinion after examining her," the doctor replied.

But destiny unfolded with a cruel swiftness. Before we could transport her to Bangalore, Gudia departed from this world. A shroud of grief enveloped us all, Shalu, unresponsive, lost in the depths of sorrow.

A pall hung over the family; each member veiled in a cloak of sorrow. Time, the elusive healer, offered no respite. They say time heals all wounds, but the indelible scars of loss remain etched in the recesses of the heart. Memories, both smiles and tears, twisted our heartstrings, refusing to be diluted by the passage of time.

The prevailing myth, that the mere march of time could mend the most profound wounds, was shattered. Time, it appeared, was not a healer but a factor in healing. Change demanded more than the ticking of the clock; it necessitated a proactive force, an agent of transformation.

In the midst of grief, a simple gesture emerged as a balm—the warmth of a hug. In that embrace, the aggrieved found solace, a respite from pain and a haven amid the storm.

And then, a glimmer of light amid the shadows—a phone call heralded a new chapter.

"Congratulations! There is good news," Laxmi's voice, after 3 years, rang through the phone.

"What happened? Have you won the lottery?" I quipped; my curiosity piqued.

"Even more than that," she teased.

"I have no patience now; please tell me immediately," I urged.

"Shalu is expecting now," she revealed.

"Wow, this is great news!" I exulted in excitement.

Yet, shadows of negativity loomed over me, a sudden descent from joy to sorrow.

"What happened? Why the silence?" Laxmi probed.

"Nothing," I evaded.

"Please tell me, are you not happy about this news?" she persisted.

"I am truly happy for Shalu and praying to God that everything should be smooth and good. The baby must be healthy enough," I assured.

"I can understand, and I'm thinking the same thing," she whispered. "God is great, and everything will be intact. We will go to the temple in the evening to pray."

"Sure!" I agreed.

And then, the day arrived when we received the much-awaited news.

"Congratulations, papa, you have become Nanaji to a baby boy!" Deepak's voice conveyed the jubilant announcement.

"Thank-you, and congrats to you and the whole family!" I exclaimed with joy.

"How is the baby, and how is Shalu?" I inquired.

"Both are alright, don't worry," Deepak reassured.

"Beta, how is the baby?" My voice quivered with emotion.

"He is also fine and in good health," he affirmed.

"We are coming in the evening," I declared.

This news painted smiles across our faces. Trembling hands cradled the child as I held him in my lap. By the grace of God, the milestones of his birth unfurled seamlessly, and as we celebrated his first birthday, a sense of peace settled over our minds.

Now, the boy named Krish had turned 6, accompanying us to celebrate the marriage anniversary of his Nana and Nani.

"Have we reached the hospital?" Babli's question pierced through my reverie.

"Oh, not yet. It is a toll booth," I responded.

"Papa, I will come with you," Vicky entered the ambulance.

"Why have you come here, beta? We are about to reach it now," I said.

"I can't sit there without mummy," he insisted. "Mamma, how are you feeling now?"

"I am OK, don't worry," Laxmi reassured, a smile gracing her lips at the sight of her beloved son.

"Right, Mamma. I will sit with you now," Vicky declared.

"Come to me," Laxmi beckoned.

As the present unfolded, my thoughts meandered back to a promise made in the past.

"All have quit cigarettes except you, papa," Vicky had observed one day, departing for Hyderabad to attend college in Bidar.

"No, beta. I will also quit," I declared.

"It is not possible; I can bet," he challenged.

"OK, you have only 6 months left in Bidar, right?" I reminded him.

"Yes," he affirmed.

"Today, I promise that I will quit smoking before you come back here finally," I vowed.

"Let's see. I don't have faith in this," he remained sceptical.

"You will see this time," I reassured.

And it happened I quit smoking in June, while he returned in July.

Amid the tumultuous times, the absence of campus interviews due to recession led Vicky to ponder alternative paths.

"Shall I join HCL BPO, papa?" he proposed one day.

"Why BPO?" I questioned, surprised.

"There's no job for me in any company. They insist if I join BPO, they will shift me to the technical side as soon as the opportunity occurs," Vicky explained.

"Okay, it's better to keep yourself busy than sitting idle," I responded, attempting to infuse a sense of optimism into the conversation.

"Right, papa. I will start working there for now," Vicky acquiesced.

Six months elapsed, and he left the BPO company, drawn by the allure of Wipro's promise to transition him to a technical role after 1.5 years. Time fluttered away, elusive and unpredictable. Vicky, however, struggled to secure a job aligned with his qualifications, a frustration compounded by the looming spectre of education loan EMIs.

"Vicky is 28 now. When should we look for a girl for him?" Laxmi pondered one day; the weight of concern etched on her face.

"I don't think he will agree at this stage because of his service and income," I replied, trying to temper her worries.

"It's true, but his age is advancing. If we wait longer, he will be in his thirties, and it will be difficult to find a girl for him," Laxmi voiced her apprehension.

"I know, but what can we do?" I sighed.

"There is a girl in our office who looks very innocent. Shall I talk to her father?" I proposed one day, as Laxmi persistently advocated for Vicky's marriage.

"What's her caste?" Laxmi inquired.

"She is also Sharma," I revealed.

"Talk to her father first, and then call them for lunch," Laxmi suggested.

"Okay, but firstly ask Vicky," I insisted.

"I don't want to get married while earning this income, mummy. Why don't you understand?" Vicky resisted his mother's persistence.

"Who's that girl?" my sister queried, joining the conversation.

"She is a very good girl and is in our office. She looks very innocent," I described.

"Then call them. We are also looking for a good girl for our grandson," she urged.

"Sure, Bahanji. We will inform you when they plan to come," I assured her.

Deepti, the innocent girl from our office, arrived for lunch one Sunday with her parents. Laxmi, quick to form impressions, exclaimed, "She is a very good girl" upon Deepti's arrival.

"Bahanji, come immediately. She is a very good girl," Laxmi phoned my sister.

Bahanji and the boy's parents arrived within half an hour and expressed approval for Deepti. Destiny, however, had a different script. A call from the boy's father revealed a mismatch in their astrological charts, bringing an abrupt end to the match.

Despite the unforeseen turn of events, Deepti and her parents remained eager to unite her with Vicky. Fate had other plans, and Deepti became my daughter, addressing me with respect as "Paa." She eventually married a colleague from our office, and we, Laxmi and me, performed the kanyadan, welcoming them into their new life.

In the midst of these memories, the ambulance driver's voice penetrated the recesses of my thoughts.

"We reached the hospital, Sahib!" the driver announced.

"Oh yes, immediately bring the stretcher, please," I responded.

And so, after 8 hours in the ambulance, we emerged into the present. A lifetime lived within those 8 hours, an odyssey etched in memory, unforgettable until my last breath.

Never did I fathom…the true essence of life resides in the challenges of each passing day. It's not merely about tears or smiles; life unfolds as a treasure trove. Family, friends, career, health, failures—each element contributes to this kaleidoscope. Instead of bemoaning what we lack, pay heed to the small joys. I practiced this philosophy during the so-called hard times.

Remember, at the end of each day, you are crafting your own story. Life, for me, should be a narrative worth living and, perhaps, worth dying for.

Life ought to be vibrant, filled with colours! Each hue deserves to be seen and savoured individually, for when they blend, the tapestry becomes a monochromatic black. Red, yellow, green, and orange—these colours should coexist side by side, each contributing to the collective beauty. In life, too, different roles played by the same individual should exist harmoniously, separate but not conflicting. A father ought not to carry his paternal duties into the office, just as a politician should prioritise leadership over familial roles.

In ancient India, this concept was termed 'varnashram'—an expectation that everyone, irrespective of their role, would engage with enthusiasm. The blending of professions proved counterproductive.

For this reason, I opted for Voluntary Retirement from Indian Express, prioritising the health of my beloved wife, who often found herself alone at home due to my erratic timings.

If a doctor wishes to venture into business, let him run a separate enterprise, secondary to his primary profession, and avoid commodifying medicine. Maintaining these mental 'containers' as distinct entities is the secret to a contented life.

Laxmi's life, by contrast, unfolded as a tapestry of trials and triumphs. Married at the tender age of 18, she swiftly embraced the responsibilities of a large family. Her parents departed early in her life, and familial upheavals necessitated the displacement of her childhood home.

Tragedy struck again when her younger sister and brother passed away at a young age. Her granddaughter's untimely departure left hearts shattered.

Post the marriage of her daughter, Laxmi grappled with a severe illness but triumphed over adversity. Now, with a fractured leg and an impending surgery, she remains undaunted.

And yet, in the face of these challenges, one could never fathom her tribulations. Her strong willpower and unwavering positivity have turned hardship into triumph. We pray for her continued health, aspiring for her to serve as an inspiration for us all—she, indeed, is my inspiration.

This isn't the conclusion of the story but merely the end of the ambulance journey. There is much more awaiting, a continuation of the tale...

& Beyond

The sterile white walls of the hospital seemed to close in as I approached the reception desk, urgency etched on my face. "Sister, please call the doctor for a check-up of my wife," I implored after swiftly admitting her to the emergency ward.

"Oh sure, please sit and wait!" replied the nurse, her tone calm amidst the underlying tension.

Time crawled during the 20-minute wait until the doctor finally entered the emergency ward, seeking the patient. After a meticulous examination, he prescribed a battery of tests.

"Please come with me," the receptionist instructed. "Your wife will be admitted here for an operation. She will be shifted to the ward tomorrow morning. Here is the estimate; please deposit money at the cash counter," she added, her words hanging in the air.

"OK, we will," I managed to respond.

"Jijaji, please eat something," Babli, my sister-in-law, pleaded.

"No, I don't feel hungry," I dismissed the notion.

"Please, Jijaji. Didi is feeling better now after the injection. If you don't eat, Vicky won't eat either," Babli reasoned, concern etched on her face.

Despite my worries for Laxmi, Babli had arranged food from her home, bringing it after a quick call to her family in Noida.

I fretted about Laxmi. The impending operation loomed large, and the prospect of managing everything alone conjured memories of the critical situation after Shalu's marriage.

"Vicky, you go home. I am here with Laxmi," I suggested after finally succumbing to a meal.

"No, papa, you go. I won't even sleep at home," Vicky insisted.

"Don't be adamant, please go," I urged.

"You may go, papa. I won't even sleep at home," he repeated.

"OK, we both will remain here," I conceded.

The next day, a doctor summoned me to accompany him.

"Yes, doctor, is everything alright? I hope there is no complication," I queried, my anxiety palpable.

"Nothing much, but we have to operate on her leg. The bones are crushed at 3 places. We will insert a plate during the operation," the doctor explained.

"OK, but will she be able to walk after that?" I asked, seeking a glimmer of reassurance.

"We think so, but first, allow us to operate on her," he responded.

"Please go ahead," I conceded in a sombre tone.

"We will operate in the morning. In the meantime, we will give her some medicine. Ask her not to eat anything after dinner," the doctor instructed.

"OK," I replied, caught in the ebb and flow of emotions.

As the day unfolded, my sister Pushpa arrived at the hospital, a beacon of support.

"What happened, Vinod?" she inquired, her concern evident.

"She will be operated on tomorrow," I informed her.

"But how could it be so serious? Had she slipped somewhere? You all went to celebrate your anniversary, isn't it?" she pondered.

"No, she hadn't slipped, but her foot bent on the stairs, and 3 fractures were detected," I explained.

"It's really surprising. Don't you worry; everything will be alright," she reassured, her affectionate demeanour providing solace.

In the hospital room, tears welled not only in our eyes but in everyone's. The outpouring of love and sympathy for Laxmi was palpable. The news of her accident was met with disbelief, the notion of 3 fractures from a mere foot bending seeming implausible.

"Please keep her ready. The nurse will come in half an hour to prepare her for the operation," the doctor instructed during the morning check-up.

"Alright, doctor!" I acknowledged.

"Don't you worry; you will go there and get relieved of all your leg pain," I consoled Laxmi.

"OK," she uttered.

In the hospital room, with Vicky, Shalu, Babli, and Pushpa didi, we awaited the nurse's arrival to escort Laxmi to the operating room.

"How are you, Aunty?" the nurse asked upon entering the room.

"I am alright!" Laxmi responded.

"Shall we go?" the nurse asked.

"OK," Laxmi confirmed.

We encircled Laxmi until the gate of the operating room, sharing smiles to lift her spirits before entering.

"See you, my love. Now go to the room.", I said.

"It will take more than 4 hours for the operation and observation room," the doctor advised.

"No, doctor, we will sit outside the operating room," I insisted.

"It is not allowed. You may inquire about the status at a phone number. We will inform you," the doctor replied.

Reluctantly, we returned to the room, a heavy silence hanging over us.

"Today is the England-India match, Vicky," I remarked.

"Hmm," Vicky responded.

"Let's go to the waiting room and watch the match," I suggested.

The proposal prompted surprise and questioning looks, as if I had lost my senses. How could a person, whose wife was in the operating room for a major procedure, think of a cricket match at that moment? Anger flickered on their faces.

"If we sit here, our attention cannot be diverted, and we will be stressed without any results. However, if we watch the match, the stress may come down a little. I am equally concerned about what is happening in the operating room, but sitting idle or watching a match to pass time doesn't make any difference," I explained.

The rationale brought a modicum of understanding, yet doubts lingered about whether we should go to the waiting room.

"Right, papa, let's go, but I will ask about the status by phone every 15 minutes," Vicky suggested.

"OK," I agreed.

"Please come into the operating room," a technician requested during one of the follow-up calls.

We hastened to the room.

"How was the operation, doctor? Is it over?" we inquired eagerly.

"It is successful, but you have to counsel the patient. She is stressed that her leg is not felt," the doctor explained.

"OK, can we meet her?" I asked, yearning to assure Laxmi.

"Not yet please wait for half an hour. If we can persuade her that her leg is very much there and not amputated, then only you will be allowed to meet her, but only one person," the doctor replied.

"OK, doctor, thank-you," I acknowledged, the waiting game continuing in the sterile corridors of the hospital.

In the intricate tapestry of life, I often find myself harbouring an unsettling apprehension amid moments of joy. A peculiar prayer escapes my lips, a plea to the cosmos that this fleeting period of happiness may remain undisturbed, shielded from the unforeseen storms that tend to accompany euphoria.

This pattern has woven itself into the fabric of my existence. Each occasion of jubilation seems entangled with an unseen sorrow, a subtle reminder that life's equilibrium maintains a delicate dance.

This paradox manifested itself glaringly when Shalu embarked on her matrimonial journey. The joyous occasion of her wedding was swiftly overshadowed by an unexpected turmoil, as narrated above.

The anticipation of celebrating our 25th wedding anniversary was thwarted by unforeseen circumstances. In 2012, when our children orchestrated a grand anniversary fete, an enigmatic tempest awaited its moment. Laxmi, my wife, suffered a severe leg fracture, leading to an operation and an extended period of bed rest lasting over 6 months.

"Jijaji, didi will accompany us to Noida since there's no one to care for her at home," Babli informed me, a sentiment that offered a modicum of relief.

I harbour no resentment toward the divine for this juxtaposition of joy and sorrow in my life. Invariably, a guardian emerges, a saviour dispatched by fate to ease my tribulations.

History repeated itself when Laxmi faced paralysis, compelling Babli to bring her home. Once again, during Laxmi's surgery and subsequent convalescence, Babli emerged as the harbinger of relief.

Babli, a providential figure, consistently appears in our lives, extending aid not only to us but to anyone fortunate enough to cross her path.

"Do you have any objection, Jijaji?" Babli inquired.

"No, Babli, I harbour no objection. You've always been my solace. Yet, you're undertaking the noble task of sheltering a bedridden individual. Not everyone possesses the virtue to perform such an altruistic act," I expressed.

"You're overthinking. Don't dwell; otherwise, your empty head will ache soon," she jested, a momentary respite amid the gravity of the situation.

Reluctantly, Laxmi hesitated but eventually agreed to accompany Babli to her home. Our weekly visits and daily conversations bridged the physical distance.

"Why don't we visit mummy every other day, papa?" Vicky questioned.

"Understand, my son. Frequent visits may disrupt their family life and privacy," I explained.

"No, papa, you're lying. You don't want to go because you don't love mummy anymore," Vicky accused, his disappointment evident.

"I wish to be with her every second of my life, beta, but visiting their house frequently isn't feasible," I tried to reason.

"Don't talk to me," Vicky retorted in anger.

"Manoj, we will take her back now," I informed him during a visit to Max for a regular check-up.

"Why? She's still not fit. Who will take care of her?" Manoj questioned.

"My sister will come home to take care," I reassured.

"Okay, but this isn't ideal for her. Do you have any grievances during her stay at our home?" he asked.

"No, please don't talk like that. I am truly indebted forever to find a person like you in my life," I expressed.

After 1.5 months of her operation, Laxmi returned home, transforming our abode back into a haven. Her absence had rendered our dwelling a mere place for sleep, filled with a palpable sorrow that vanished upon her return.

In problem-solving, the best solutions often emerge not from rigorous contemplation but from nurturing peaceful thoughts. Leave room for the divine to intervene. Everyone eagerly awaited Laxmi's homecoming, visiting and extending warm wishes. Gradually, with consistent physiotherapy, her condition improved. With indomitable willpower, she learned to walk unassisted, a triumphant moment for all. Babli and Shalu stood as pillars of strength throughout her convalescence.

Life, an ever-changing landscape, witnessed about a year of mutual care and support. In that time, we evolved into a genuinely happy family, cherishing each other.

Around mid-2013, Vicky approached us with a proposition. A friend named Shiva was set to visit for lunch on a Sunday. Vicky, being Vicky, left the choice of the menu to Laxmi, assuring her that anything she prepared would be delightful. Shalu and Babli were also invited, and the day unfolded with warmth and camaraderie.

After Shiva's departure, Vicky approached us with a revelation. "I want to tell you something, papa and mummy," he began.

"Go ahead, please," Laxmi encouraged.

"How was the girl, mummy?" Vicky inquired.

"She was good. What do you mean? Do you like her? Where is she from, and what about her parents?" Laxmi questioned anxiously.

"Just a minute, mummy. Okay, I like her and want to pursue this relationship if you permit," Vicky declared.

"We have no objection, beta," I assured him. "However, we'd like to interact with her family. If everything is good, we will proceed."

This moment marked a departure for Vicky, who had never asked for anything. We didn't wish to disappoint him. He called the girl immediately, conveying our approval, and urged her to bring her parents for a meeting. It was revealed that she hailed from Kullu, a Himalayan town.

Amid the buoyant atmosphere of impending celebration, a discerning eye could catch the subtle nuances of Laxmi's demeanour. A quiet sadness lingered beneath her facade of normalcy; a fact not lost on me. I probed gently, but she brushed off my concern, insisting she was fine. Yet, the shadows of unspoken thoughts played upon her countenance.

As the evening unfolded and Manoj arrived, his perceptive eyes mirrored my observations. Sensing her melancholy, he invited her for a stroll, a simple gesture that carried the weight of profound concern.

"Why the melancholy, didi?" queried Manoj as they strolled down the street.

"Nothing, Manoj, I am content," she asserted.

"Then why wear the mask of sorrow?" His inquiry unveiled her true emotions. She wept, confessing a reluctance toward Vicky marrying outside our caste. It seemed a minor concern, one that could have been dismissed with a simple 'no.' However, the prospect of shattering our son's joyous anticipation tugged at our hearts. His happiness was so cherished, no one dared to mar it.

Wisdom dictates leaving certain matters to destiny, trusting that whatever unfolds is ultimately for our good. This perspective offered a temporary solace, yet divine plans have a way of unfolding, indifferent to human predictions.

"Mummy, Shiva called today," Shalu shared one day.

"What did she say?" Laxmi inquired.

"We had a general conversation. I mentioned that my mummy is a very simple lady, and after marriage, you'll have to take care of her," Shalu replied.

"And what did she say?" Laxmi pressed.

"She assured me she would take care. However, she added that if anyone criticises her twice, she wouldn't tolerate it and would respond with the same behaviour. It's just her nature," Shalu relayed.

"That's quite serious, Shalu. Such behaviour indicates either straightforwardness or cunningness. It's not a positive sign," Laxmi discerned.

"Yes, mummy, I was taken aback too. How will she manage with you after marriage? You tend to keep quiet after every incident, and this might affect your health," Shalu expressed her concerns.

Laxmi's countenance grew grave after hearing this revelation. Seeking counsel, she shared the details with me.

"Don't worry; we'll talk to her. Sometimes, they fail to comprehend the responsibilities that come after marriage," I reassured Laxmi.

"Papa, Shiva's parents are coming to meet you this Sunday," Vicky informed me one day.

"Alright, we'll meet them and discuss their customs. Be at home," I instructed.

"Okay, papa."

I discussed the impending meeting with Deepak Ji and Manoj, both of whom promised to attend and offer their insights.

"Namaskar, Sharma Ji," Shiva's parents greeted us upon arrival.

"Namaskar, please come and sit," we welcomed them.

"Shiva told me about Ankit and your family, Sharma Ji," her father initiated.

"Yes, we met her; she seems like a good girl," I acknowledged.

"To be straightforward, when children like each other, we should agree to their marriage first," her father proposed.

"Yes, I agree," I concurred.

"Who else is in your family?" I inquired.

"Me, my wife, my 2 sons, Shiva, and my mother. She is quite old," he replied.

"Alright. In our family, there's me, my wife, our daughter Shalu, her husband Deepak, her son Krish, and Ankit. A small family," I shared.

"If everything looks good, shall we start the rituals?" he asked.

"Which rituals? We need to discuss many things," I clarified. "We can't perform the engagement ceremony like this. None of our family members are present."

"No issues, we'll do it later. But the wedding will take place in Kullu since my mother is very old and can't travel this far," her father insisted.

"My wife isn't keeping well and can't travel to a hilly place. Let's do the engagement ceremony in Kullu, and the wedding can happen in Delhi," I suggested.

"No, no, it's not possible," he rejected.

"Let's reconsider," his wife suggested.

"No, if the wedding has to happen here, then you come and make the arrangements; I won't attend," he declared.

His adamant stance left us all surprised. Such discussions should have occurred within their home, requiring no immediate action from our side. After their departure, they left behind a tense and unpleasant atmosphere.

Shiva's father's unwavering stance, disliked by everyone, prompted my wife to suggest reconsidering the proposal.

"Is it that simple? Our beloved son is involved, and this is a delicate matter. Love is so blind that he won't agree to it," I argued.

"Then go ahead and do whatever they say," she replied angrily.

"Understand one thing. Our son is extraordinary, and he has made numerous sacrifices for the family. We can't make decisions about his life in isolation. Don't worry; I will talk to him. If he doesn't agree, we'll be left with no option but to proceed with the marriage to that girl. I've observed him; he looks very sad," I explained.

The atmosphere remained tense for a week after the visit of Shiva's parents.

"Sit, Vicky; I want to discuss something with you," I requested one day after the incident.

"Yes, papa."

"You're aware of everything that has transpired. We're not against that girl, but the behaviour of her parents and her conversation with Shalu is concerning," I expressed.

He remained silent.

"At least tell me your perspective on this?" I asked.

"It's alright, papa. If you don't like them, say no to her father," he murmured.

"It's not about what I or you like. It's about your whole life," I emphasised.

"I'm doing everything for the family's well-being, and if all of you don't approve, there's no point in marrying a girl who doesn't fit into our family," he asserted.

"Alright, I'll inform her father that we're declining the proposal. But please don't be sad and upset. We'll find the best solution for you," I assured.

"Okay, I'm going," and with that, he left.

Time had woven its intricate threads since the fateful incident that left us in quiet contemplation. I decided to make the call, a diplomatic endeavour to bridge the gap between 2 families standing on divergent grounds. Dialling the number with practiced ease, I politely recounted the intricate dynamics that had unfolded, 2 families entwined in a delicate dance of differences. However, his response was curt - a dismissive "OK" that hung in the air, concluding the conversation abruptly.

But did the matter truly end there? I believe that was merely the prologue. The task of restoring normalcy to the family atmosphere loomed, a challenge not easily surmountable. We entrusted the reins to the hands of time and the divine.

Three months passed, each family member navigating their daily routines, maintaining a facade of normalcy while the echoes of that incident lingered beneath the surface. Laxmi, breaking the silence, broached the subject one day.

"It's been a while. Should we talk to Vicky about finding a suitable match?" she suggested.

"It's a delicate matter," I replied. "I'll attempt it."

Summoning Vicky for a heart-to-heart conversation, I initiated a dialogue one day.

"Vicky, come sit here," I beckoned.

"Yes, papa."

"How's your work going?" I inquired.

"Normal, papa. Nothing new," he responded.

"I think we should look for a suitable match for you," I suggested.

"Hmm," he acknowledged.

"Can we go ahead?" I probed further.

"As you wish, papa," he acquiesced.

As my hand rested on his shoulder, a floodgate of emotions burst forth. Tears welled in his eyes, and he wept inconsolably.

"Don't worry, beta. I am with you always. If you believe living without her is impossible, I will proceed with the marriage, regardless of others' opinions," I consoled him.

"Give me some time, papa. I will do what's best for the family. Everything will be alright," he assured.

"Take your time—whether a month, 2, or 6. Reflect and let me know your decision," I granted.

"Okay, papa."

To nurture enthusiasm, one must harbour faith in the inherent goodness of life, in the original goodness dwelling within oneself and others. Regardless of life's trials, one should believe that behind the dark curtain of adversity lies a concealed lesson or an unforeseen blessing.

Regret and grudges, like toxins, erode joy and well-being, especially in the later stages of life. Ageing individuals, poised to serve as mentors, find these negative emotions hindering their potential to be inspiring examples.

Regret often manifests as sadness, guilt, or disappointment over past actions. While everyone makes regrettable decisions, dwelling on them exacerbates the distress, akin to angry bees buzzing incessantly within the mind.

In the early days of 2014, I broached a crucial topic with Vicky. "Vicky, I want to ask you something."

"Yes, papa, tell me. Do you want something?" he queried.

"Yes, Vicky. I want to know whether we should look for a match for you now, if you're okay with it," I proposed.

"Hmm, okay, papa, as you wish," he responded.

"Are you genuinely not angry with your papa?" I questioned.

"No, papa," he reassured, embracing me. He glanced at his mother and confirmed with a smile, "You may go ahead as you wish."

"Thank-you so much, beta. You've given us immense relief. God bless you always," we expressed our gratitude.

In the interim, Laxmi dialled Shalu and Babli in excitement. For the first time in a while, her face radiated relaxation and joy. A festival spirit engulfed our home. After enduring a prolonged period of despair, happiness had finally returned.

One day, I approached Mr. Shukla, the secretary of a Brahmin Patrika in our area, who often visited for subscription and casual conversations.

"Shukla Ji, please recommend a suitable girl for our son," I requested.

"I know several girls, but it would be better if you share Ankit's biodata in the magazine. Numerous eligible boys and girls appear there, giving you the option to find a suitable match," Shukla Ji suggested.

"Okay, I'll share Ankit's details with you. Please include them in your magazine," I agreed.

I registered Ankit on various matrimonial sites, including Brahmin Patrika. Additionally, I reached out to relatives and acquaintances, seeking recommendations for a compatible match. Excitement filled the air, as happiness knocked at our door after a prolonged absence.

One day, a call disrupted the routine. "Could I speak to Mr. Vinod Sharma?"

"Yes, speaking!"

"My name is Hari Shankar Sharma, calling from Sector 10 Vasundhara. I've seen the biodata of your son and would like to visit your place."

"When do you want to meet?" I inquired.

"Can I come within half an hour?" he asked.

"Yes, you can come. Please bring the girl's photo and her kundli," I instructed.

"Okay, I am coming."

Exactly half an hour later, the doorbell chimed, announcing Mr. Sharma's arrival.

"Welcome, Sharma Ji. Please come and sit," I welcomed him, and he came accompanied by his wife.

"How are you? Where did you come across this information?" I asked.

"I am a subscriber of Brahmin Patrika and read the details of your son," he disclosed.

"Okay. Is she your daughter?" I inquired.

"No, she is my niece, my elder brother's youngest daughter," he clarified.

"Where is her father, and where does he reside?" I continued my inquiry.

"He resides in Mathura," he answered.

"Who else is in his family?" I probed.

"This is the youngest daughter. She has 3 elder sisters and one elder brother, all of whom are married," he shared.

"Sounds good. What is she doing? Is she working?" I asked.

"Yes, she is B.Ed. and working in a nearby school," he revealed.

"Tell me something about your family, Sharma Ji," he prompted.

"I have 2 children. My daughter is older and married, and my son is Ankit. This is our small family," I conveyed.

"Did you bring a photo of the girl?" I questioned.

"No, I forgot. I will send it via email shortly," he said.

Within 10 minutes, a photo of the girl arrived in our inbox. A single glance, and everyone was captivated by her charm.

"We all liked her at first sight. Ankit also said yes to her photo," I declared.

"We want to meet the girl," I expressed.

"Sure, Sharma Ji. We will arrange a meeting at our home and inform you. We'll bring the girl and other relatives here," he assured.

"Okay, inform me about the date and time to meet the girl and her parents," I instructed.

In the vibrant tapestry of life, where each relationship is a delicate thread, we constantly find ourselves testing the boundaries, akin to a young French chef managing her team. Her words lingered in my mind - "They are like children; they test your limits."

Relationships, I pondered, are intricately woven around the boundaries 2 individuals carve out for themselves. It's a dance of give and take, a delicate negotiation where you keep pushing and pulling until a space emerges, settling the relationship. The question lies in how much one is willing to endure, where one draws the line.

Marriage, I realised, is no exception. It's a subtle game of pushing limits, a test of endurance and tolerance. The challenge is not about who defines their boundaries first; it's a mutual exploration of each other's limits and one's own capacity. It beckons the question - what can you endure, and what's non-negotiable?

The phone call from the uncle of the girl, a calligraphy of fate, marked a significant turn. "Sharma ji, tomorrow is Sunday. I talked to my elder brother, who is also keen to meet you people. Can you come to our home tomorrow?" he inquired, setting the stage for a pivotal meeting.

"Yes, Mr. Sharma, we will come. I will talk to my daughter and son-in-law and will inform you," I responded, a surge of anticipation coursing through my veins.

Excitement rippled through our home as I shared the news with Shalu. "Shalu, there is good news," I declared.

"Yes, papa, are we going to meet the girl?" she asked eagerly.

"Yes, we will go there tomorrow. Can you come today evening? We will prepare for the same. I am also talking to Deepak Ji just now," I shared the excitement in my voice.

"Yes, papa, I will definitely come today to discuss further," she affirmed before hanging up.

The eve of the much-anticipated day arrived, with our home buzzing with excitement. Shalu, Deepak, Krish, Manoj, Babli, Abhishek, and Prerna gathered, a collective excitement echoing through the walls. The prospect of meeting the potential bride had cast a spell, and together we embarked on the short journey of 1.5 kilometres to their home.

"Welcome, Sharma ji," greeted Mr. Sharma, the uncle, ushering us warmly into their abode. "Meet my elder brother, Priyanka's father, her mother, and other family members," he continued, introducing us to the eager family.

Once the initial greetings subsided, Shalu, our vocal representative, broached the subject. "Can we meet the girl?" she asked after exchanging pleasantries with the girl's parents and relatives.

"Yes, of course. She is coming, here she comes."

All eyes converged on Priyanka as she entered the room, a general affirmation emanating from the glint in everyone's eyes. "Namaste," she greeted, gracefully taking her place on the sofa.

The ladies initiated a conversation, delving into topics like qualifications and hobbies. Deepak, ever the facilitator, turned to Vicky. "Vicky, please talk to her if you want."

"No, Jiju, it's alright," Vicky replied shyly.

"No, beta, you people can go inside the room and talk to each other. Maybe the girl wants to ask you something," someone suggested, breaking the tension with laughter.

After a private conversation, Vicky emerged, and all eyes turned to him for the verdict. "Yes, Vicky?" I inquired.

"I will inform you," he replied.

Deepak and Manoj, the wise counsellors, accompanied Vicky outside for a more in-depth discussion. After a brief deliberation, they returned with the news: it was a resounding YES from our side.

A wave of joy swept through the entire family. Immediately, plans were set in motion to fix a date for the Roka ceremony in Agra. The decision received unanimous approval, and the celebration mode was officially activated.

However, as life would have it, joyous moments can be interrupted by unforeseen events. Laxmi, despite the jubilation, complained of a severe headache and chest pain that evening. Concerned, we sought medical advice, visiting a nearby hospital where her symptoms were attributed to high blood pressure or gastric issues.

As the night unfolded, Laxmi found no relief, and the decision was made to consult our family doctor, Dr. Ganesh, the next day. His recommendation for an echo raised concerns.

"What's the report, doctor?" I asked anxiously.

"It seems there's an issue with the heart. Consult with a cardiologist," he advised.

The following day, we found ourselves in the capable hands of Dr. Parneesh Arora at Fortis Hospital, Noida. His urgent directive was clear: "Immediately take her to OT."

The gravity of the situation sent shivers down my spine. "What happened, doctor? Is anything serious?" I asked.

"She has had a heart attack and needs immediate angiography," he explained.

The word "heart attack" hung in the air like an ominous cloud. "Don't worry, you have come on time. I will see to it," reassured the doctor.

The hours that followed were tense, but Dr. Arora's expertise prevailed. "She is out of danger now," he informed us. Angioplasty, accompanied by the placement of a stent, had been performed.

"We have placed one stent now and will keep her under observation. If a second stent is required, we will give it the day after tomorrow," he declared.

After the prescribed rest and a second stent placement, Laxmi was declared fit. "You can take her home. We are discharging her today," the doctor confirmed after 3 days.

"Can she leave home now?" I inquired.

"No, she should step out of the house only after a week's rest," he advised.

The impending Roka ceremony, initially planned with a journey to Agra, had to be reconsidered in light of Laxmi's health. The decision to hold the ceremony at Priyanka's uncle's place nearby was made, ensuring Laxmi's comfort.

As the familial celebrations unfolded, life had once again reminded us of its unpredictability.

The air in the house buzzed with palpable excitement as Shalu stepped in, brimming with enthusiasm. Her brother's wedding rituals were on the horizon, and she was determined to make every moment memorable.

"Mummy, what do you think of giving to the girl tomorrow?" Shalu queried, her eyes sparkling with anticipation. Laxmi, her mother, pondered the question, knowing the significance of the occasion.

"I believe we should present her with a set and a sari, accompanied by a shagun envelope. And, of course, sweets and fruits," Laxmi responded, her mind already weaving through the details.

"Sounds good," Shalu agreed. "Let's make a list of the items to be carried tomorrow."

Babli also entered home in the meanwhile.

As the trio engaged in nonstop discussions, laughter, and planning, I observed the animated exchange. Their faces radiated a glow as if they had just returned from the most indulgent parlour session.

The following day unfolded with peaceful rituals, a cascade of celebrations, and the melody of music. Calls were made to siblings, inviting them to join in the joyous occasion. Manoj, with his foresight, had arranged for dhol wallas, and soon, the house resonated with the rhythmic beats, drawing everyone into the spirited dance.

"We'd also love to visit your home in Mathura, Sharma ji," I proposed, extending the joyous camaraderie.

"Sure, but please come with all your family members next Sunday to Agra, where we have our other relatives. We have a banquet hall and a hotel there. You may like to see where the wedding ceremony will be solemnised. We'll also discuss the marriage date since there's some work being done in the locality in Mathura," Sharma ji suggested.

"It depends on Laxmi's health. However, we'll inform you," I conveyed after conferring with the family.

The homecoming marked the commencement of a jubilant celebration. The long-awaited day had finally arrived, ushering in a renewed sense of happiness.

"So, can we go next Sunday?" I asked Laxmi. "Do you feel like travelling?"

"I am alright now and can go anywhere," came her energetic reply, sending ripples of laughter through the room.

"Deepak Ji, please arrive at 9 am tomorrow. We'll head to Agra on time so that we can return promptly," I instructed over the phone.

"Sure, we will be there," Deepak Ji affirmed.

Sunday dawned with contagious happiness as our family, Shalu's family, and Babli's family embarked on the journey to Agra in 3 cars.

After lively discussions, persuasive arguments, and shared laughter, a decision crystallised: the wedding would be solemnised on the 30th of November 2014 in Agra itself. The engagement and ring ceremony were scheduled for the 26th of November in Vasundhara. The plans were set, and we returned home, immersed in the festive spirit.

Preparations were underway, with Laxmi actively participating in shopping and other arrangements despite her recent health concerns. The engagement venue was booked, and the entire household resonated with celebratory vibes. Little did we know that destiny had its own plans.

"Vicky, I've been feeling some ache in my left-hand and heaviness in my chest for the last few days," I confided one day, a shadow cast over the hustle and bustle of wedding preparations.

"Since when, papa?" Vicky inquired.

"For about a week. I thought it was due to some heavy food, and I took Eno last night, but there's still some heaviness. I also had some left-hand pain last night, so I took a painkiller," I explained.

"What are you doing, papa? Why didn't you tell me last night? What if something happened?" Vicky scolded me. "Come now, we're going to Fortis Noida for an ECG."

"No beta, there's no need. I'm fine, and we also have more bookings to do," I insisted.

"Nothing doing, you're coming with me. What's the harm in getting the ECG done? If everything is alright, then we'll go for the bookings on our way back," Vicky decided.

"OK," I reluctantly agreed, knowing there was little room for negotiation.

"What's the report, doctor?" I asked after the ECG.

"Nothing wrong, but we need to do an ECHO," the doctor replied.

"Is everything okay, doctor?" Vicky queried with a quiver in his voice.

"Yes, it's okay, but we found some inconsistency in the ECG, so we advised an ECHO," the doctor explained.

"Okay, go ahead," Vicky confirmed.

"Papa, they want to go for angiography. They have some doubts," Vicky conveyed after some time.

"But it will take time, and your mummy is alone at home and will be worried," I voiced my concerns.

"It won't take much time. I'll inform her accordingly," Vicky assured.

"Okay."

"Papa, I've told Babli didi to take mummy along to Noida," Vicky shared after some time.

"What happened? Why are you sending her? There's a lot of work at home," I questioned.

"Papa, the doctor has advised bypass surgery," Vicky dropped the bombshell.

"What? It's not possible, Vicky. I'm feeling alright. Let's go home," I was in shock.

"I also talked to Dr. Parneesh. He himself is admitted because of surgery for appendix," Vicky informed.

I was admitted to the hospital. Dr. Parneesh recommended surgery at Fortis Escorts in Okhla and personally spoke to the senior surgeon.

I couldn't fathom it. It couldn't be possible. Shalu and Vicky visited renowned doctors, seeking second opinions. The consensus was unanimous: surgery was inevitable.

There was no turning back. The following day, I was transferred to Escorts. As I lay on the hospital bed, the realisation sank in. The major operation loomed ahead, but strangely, there was no nervousness. One thought dominated my mind - Laxmi wasn't fully recovered yet. I had to remain patient and take care of the family.

"Congratulations! The operation was successful. He will be in the observation room and will be taken to the ward tomorrow," the doctor informed the family.

Relief washed over everyone. The entire family stayed in the hospital, united in their support. I understood Laxmi's predicament and entrusted Shalu and Vicky with her care before heading to the operation theatre.

"We have to keep him for another 10 days in the hospital. Only one person can stay with him in his single room," the doctor explained.

"I'll stay with him," Vicky volunteered. Later, it was revealed that Prerna visited the hospital daily, sitting with me throughout the day. Shalu also made her way from Paschim Vihar, providing unwavering support. Although no one was allowed inside the room, their presence was a source of comfort.

Gradually, with each passing day, my strength returned, and the day arrived when I was discharged. The doctor advised 3 months of rest and lying down straight with a belt around the chest.

I felt incredibly weak, requiring assistance even for basic tasks like going to the washroom. Vicky, Shalu, along with the entire family, including Babli and Devi Behen ji, tended to my needs.

As the calendar flipped to the 12th of August, the wedding date approached, set for the 30th of November. Concerns crept in.

"Vicky, how will we manage? If my rest period concludes in November, how can I attend the marriage?" I fretted.

"It's a matter of concern, papa. We have to think about it. At present, don't think much. You are very weak. Please take rest only," Vicky advised, attempting to soothe my anxious mind. But thoughts of the impending wedding continued to linger.

In the hushed corridors of my home, a stream of people ebbed and flowed, a symphony of relations, colleagues, friends, and neighbours converging to share in the warmth of kinship. Yet, my room remained a sanctuary, off-limits to all, as per the doctor's counsel.

A call broke the monotony one day, a voice from Vicky's in-laws, expressing concern. "How are you, Sharma ji?" they inquired.

"I am alright but a bit weak," I responded.

"If you wish, we can hold the wedding in Delhi. Otherwise, we can postpone until you regain your health," they proposed kindly.

"Thank-you, Sharma ji. I will discuss with the family and inform you accordingly," I replied, contemplating the implications.

"It's not advisable for them to come to Delhi and organise the wedding. They have their own set-up in Agra," I shared with Laxmi.

"You are right. Let's talk to Shalu and consider postponing the date. Even if your rest period concludes, you are still very weak," Laxmi concurred.

"You are right. Please talk to her," I urged.

"Papa, Priyanka wants to talk to you," Vicky announced one day.

Assuming it was a conversation about my health, I took the receiver, only to be met with her uncontrollable sobs. Concern gripped me as I sought an explanation.

"What happened, beta? Why are you crying?" I inquired.

"Nothing, papa. People are talking about our relationship. First, when it was fixed, mummy fell ill, and now, when the date was fixed, you have fallen ill. If you think I am not good for your family, you can say no to me. I will not mind," she poured out in one breath.

Stunned, I remained silent. "Papa, what happened?" she pressed.

"I am sorry, beta, but whoever is telling you this, convey to them that since you entered our family, we have stayed safe and alive. Now, you, and only you, will come as my daughter to this house. Always keep this in mind," I reassured her. She fell silent. "Yes, beta, you understand what I said."

"Yes, papa, you have relieved me from pessimistic thoughts. Thank-you very much," she replied, her voice steadying.

In the tapestry of life, negative threads often threaten to unravel the fabric before any real damage occurs. A mind seasoned with wisdom and positivity has the power to envision positive outcomes, a key to overcoming adversities. The Law of Attraction suggests that worry emits negative energy into the universe, inviting a destiny steeped in ill health, strained relationships, and financial woes. Affirmations, brimming with positive wisdom, dispatch positive energy, fostering a destiny marked by success.

Negative situations, initially looming large, tend to shrink as we move forward. The secret lies in employing our innate positivity, invoking divine assistance, and leveraging a clear intellect to arrive at solutions. A powerful teaching of wisdom asserts that every situation is transient; none is permanent. To remain steadfast, resilient, and patient during challenging times is the recipe for success.

Deeply embedded in this wisdom is the understanding that every situation, regardless of its adversarial nature, harbours hidden benefits. Negative circumstances, while forging strength and wisdom, also spur creative thinking, leading to unforeseen successes and uncharted paths.

As the time for the wedding approached, discussions veered towards the postponement of the date, ultimately settling on the 25th of January 2015. The engagement venue, initially booked for the 22nd of January, fortunately, remained available.

With renewed health, my focus shifted to the intricacies of wedding preparations. Vicky, anticipating a joyous celebration, proposed a bachelor party.

"Papa, can we arrange a bachelor party where I will call my close friends and cousins?" Vicky asked one day.

"Sure, but where do you think it can be arranged?" I inquired.

"I am in touch with certain clubs that charge per member for drinks and dinner. But it's a bit costly," Vicky disclosed.

"Alright, but there is a concern," I pointed out. "You all will return late at night, and if there's an issue on the way, like the police stopping you, then?"

"Yes, papa, that is an issue. But I can't call all of them at home. There's no space, and moreover, nobody can enjoy at home," Vicky reasoned.

"Let me think," I mused.

"Why don't you arrange the bachelor party in the basement of our Noida home?" Manoj suggested to Vicky one day upon learning of the plan. "You all won't have to travel at night and can sleep there. There's ample space. You need to inform me about the number of people so I can arrange the necessary materials for the party."

"Thank-you, uncle," Vicky expressed his gratitude. "You've relieved me of all worries. That is the best place for all of us. However, don't worry about the materials; I will arrange everything."

"Don't think too much, Vicky. If you want the venue for the party to be in Noida, then I will arrange everything. No further arguments now. The matter ends," Manoj declared.

And with that, the matter concluded. The bachelor party forged a unique bond among cousins, fostering closeness that hadn't been apparent before. The worry lines eased.

Since the wedding entourage was limited to close relatives and friends for the journey to Agra, we invited most of the people to the engagement. It unfolded as a grand celebration, and many joined in the revelry.

The subsequent days were laden with various marriage-related ceremonies – ladies sangeet & mehndi on the 23rd and Bhat on the 24th. During these rituals, we discovered our family anthem. On every occasion, from Krish to myself, we recited the anthem, "Pyaar hamein kis mod pe le aaya," revelling in its joy.

On the appointed day, we set forth for Agra with family and friends. A bus was booked for the baratis, while those with cars chose to travel in their vehicles.

"Let's all go in the bus," Deepak suggested to me. "We'll all enjoy on the way. Let the cars be driven by drivers."

"That's a good idea," I agreed. "Whoever wants to come in the bus may sit. We're all going in the same bus."

Everyone, including Vicky, Shalu, and the entire family, boarded the bus. Laughter and cheer reverberated through the bus during the journey. Songs filled the air, and there was an impromptu antakshri session. Men savoured beer, creating memories that would linger as a cherished chapter in our lives.

We reached Agra on time, only to be greeted by rain. After snacks, we awaited the pause in the downpour to proceed to the banquet.

"There's water everywhere. How can we proceed to the banquet?" someone voiced their concern.

"Yes, let's wait for the rain to stop," I suggested.

The rain, however, showed no signs of relenting. The youngsters, eager to dance to the beats of the dhol, grew restless.

"Bring the dhol wallas inside. Until the rain stops, we'll enjoy it here," someone proposed.

"Right, please bring them," I agreed.

And so, the dance commenced within the confines of the hotel. After 2 hours, someone brought attention to the rain's cessation.

"See outside, there is no rain now," they observed.

"Yes, please bring the baggi," I directed.

"It can't come here because of water everywhere. We have to proceed till the banquet in buses and cars," Manoj informed.

With no other option, we began the procession. A short distance away, the baggi awaited. Vicky, his friends, and cousins leaped onto it, dancing exuberantly.

Finally, we reached the venue. As the rituals concluded, the moment of Vidai arrived. Laxmi and our sisters, having left early in the morning to prepare for the new member's welcome, awaited our return. Upon reaching home, another wave of celebration ensued.

"Priyanka, please feel free. You are like Shalu to us. We don't believe in the word 'in-law,' and hence, you are our daughter from today," I declared.

"Yes, papa," she replied, marking the beginning of a new chapter in our family saga.

In the delicate tapestry of life, it is often said that marriage marks the beginning of a new chapter for a woman. She steps into a realm where learning, understanding, application, and comportment become her companions, all in an endeavour to win hearts. Yet, contrary to conventional belief, this transformation isn't the sole journey of the bride; it extends to the entire family. Every member is obliged to embark on the journey of learning, understanding, applying, and adapting when a new member joins their familial symphony.

Priyanka, the newest entrant into our family, displayed a remarkable maturity. Hailing from a large family, she effortlessly wove understanding and camaraderie into the fabric of our lives, much like salt dissolving seamlessly in water.

The passage of time bore witness to the integration of this new member into our family. Laxmi, visibly relieved, wore the contentment on her face. Time, the ethereal concept that slips through the fingers like grains of sand, played its relentless role. The adage, "time flies when you're having fun," may echo in our ears, but time marches on, indifferent to the moments of joy or sorrow.

Life, it is said, is too short to be anything but happy. A sentiment embraced by those who have traversed the corridors of parenthood or those who have weathered the winds of advancing age. Life's brevity, an immutable reality, urges one to do well, to translate good intentions into tangible actions. Intentions, after all, stand apart from deeds as Heaven does from Hell.

There exist moments, however, where time seems to crawl at an agonizingly slow pace, each second stretching into an eternity. It is in these moments that the inexorable march of time reveals its paradox.

"What happened, Priyanka? Are you alright?" Laxmi inquired one day: her concern palpable.

"Nothing, mummy. I am feeling impulsive today. Whenever I eat something, it comes out," Priyanka shared.

"Take Eno and get some rest or go to the doctor with Vicky for a check-up," Laxmi advised.

"Nothing to worry, mummy. I will be alright."

As evening descended, Priyanka's discomfort persisted.

"Vicky, take her to the doctor," Laxmi instructed.

"What did the doctor say?" Laxmi inquired upon their return.

"She has undergone tests, and the reports will be available tomorrow. Meanwhile, she has been prescribed some medicines. Perhaps, she will be alright soon," Vicky responded.

"There is good news, mummy," Vicky announced the next day. It had been 2 years since their marriage.

"What happened? Has the report been received?" Laxmi asked.

"Yes, mummy, everything is alright. But she needs to take care and rest a little more," Vicky said.

"Okay, but what's the good news you were telling me?" Laxmi queried.

"She is pregnant."

"What? Have you told Shalu?" Laxmi asked.

"Not yet mummy. I will call her right away."

"Sister, guess what I want to tell you," Vicky exclaimed over the phone. His voice carried the excitement, and Shalu sensed it immediately.

"Tell me immediately. I can't wait any longer," Shalu urged.

"You are going to be a Bua, sister," he revealed.

"What? Are you serious? I am coming right away," Shalu responded in excitement.

Joy echoed through the household. Excitement resonated in every corner.

"We have heard some good news after a long time," Laxmi shared.

"Yes, God willing, we have to take care of her more now," I remarked.

"You are right. We will do our best for her," Laxmi agreed.

Yet, despite meticulous planning, life unfolds with its own script, written long before our entry into this world.

As days flowed seamlessly, Priyanka diligently cared for both herself and the impending arrival.

"What happened, Vicky?" Laxmi inquired after a routine check-up 3 months later.

"Nothing, mummy, everything is fine," Vicky reassured.

"Tell me the truth, Vicky. Why do you both look so sad?" Laxmi probed.

"The doctor said we need to conduct some tests. It seems there might be some complications," Vicky confessed.

"It's okay. Such things are common in this condition," Laxmi consoled.

"No, mummy, it's not normal. Anyway, we will go for the test tomorrow."

"Rest. God is great. Everything will be alright."

"The test report has come, mummy," Vicky informed after its receipt.

"What happened? Is everything alright?" Laxmi asked.

"The doctor said there is a cyst that may complicate the case. She prescribed some medicines and advised some precautions," Vicky replied.

"God will pave the way for everything. Don't worry," Laxmi assured.

Laxmi uttered words of solace to Vicky, but the emptiness in her own heart belied the reassurance. She was deeply concerned.

The following week, upon their return from the clinic, anxiety etched their faces.

"What did the doctor say?" Laxmi inquired.

"There has been a missed abortion," Vicky revealed.

"What?" She was rendered speechless for a moment.

The jubilant atmosphere that had enveloped the family just a week ago dissolved into an unexpected pall of sorrow.

In the tapestry of life, the first instance of heartbreak unfolded for Priyanka and the entire family, casting a shadow that would linger in their hearts. The little girl bore the weight of pain and loss at a tender age, and in the face of such adversity, all they could do was counsel one another, offering solace to Priyanka in particular.

Time, the great healer, worked its magic, and a semblance of normalcy returned. Vicky and Priyanka, undeterred, sought the counsel of medical expertise, undergoing tests and adhering to prescribed medications. This routine persisted for an entire year.

"I don't know, mummy, but I am very afraid," Priyanka confided one day.

"What happened, beta? Is there any problem?" Laxmi inquired.

"Actually, no problem, but I am pregnant again, and it sends shivers down my spine. What if the same thing repeats?" Priyanka expressed her worries.

"No, beta, God is very kind. We have not wronged anyone," Laxmi consoled her.

The family, once again, found themselves in a realm of dreams. Each member treaded with caution, offering extra care to Priyanka as per the doctor's advice.

"Mummy, I haven't felt anything in my stomach since morning," Priyanka revealed one day.

"Vicky, rush her to the doctor immediately," Laxmi directed.

Anxiety gripped everyone as they prayed fervently to the Almighty. Yet, their fears materialised; it was another miscarriage. Gloom enveloped the entire family, and shock held their minds captive. Priyanka slipped into depression.

"Don't worry, beta. We have done our best. This was our fate. Please don't take any tension," I uttered these words to Priyanka, fully aware that my words couldn't even provide solace to myself.

The responsibility to nurture and care for our children fell upon Laxmi and me.

"Vicky and Priyanka, don't be sad. Whatever happened and is happening in our lives is our fate. We have to bear it. Under any circumstances, we have to keep ourselves normal," I shared a story to change the mood:

A guru, imparting wisdom, addressed the challenge of maintaining balance in the face of both joy and sorrow. A disciple questioned, "How can I avoid feeling joy in my success and not feel the pain of losing a dear family member?"

The guru's response was profound, emphasising the conscious avoidance of attachment to happiness and aversion to unhappiness. These 2 elements, if unchecked, could linger long after the incident had passed, leading to sadness.

Days melted into weeks, and weeks transformed into months. Slowly, the family returned to a semblance of normalcy, yet a subtle pain lingered in the recesses of their hearts.

"Masad, I want to talk to you about something," Prerna approached me during one of their visits.

"Sure, what is it?" I responded.

"I want to talk about a boy," she revealed.

"Go on," I encouraged.

"I met him during Kriti's brother's wedding," she began. "His name is Ankit, and it seems he likes me. Kriti also mentioned the same. Ankit lives in her neighbourhood."

"Okay, do you like him too?" I asked.

"I am confused, Masad. I don't dislike him, but as of now, I'm not sure about liking him," she confessed. "Ankit expressed his desire to marry me to Kriti's father, asking them to talk to my family."

"Have you told your father?" I inquired.

"Not yet. He might get angry," she hesitated.

"No, Prerna, he is a mature person. Share your feelings with him before someone else does," I advised.

"You are right, Masad. I was very puzzled. You've relieved me," she said.

"I've seen a boy for Prerna," Manoj informed me one day.

"Alright, what does he do, and how is his family?" I questioned.

"He comes from a small family. He is the only son, working in a private company. His elder sister is married and settled in the UK," Manoj explained.

"That's good. How is the boy? Have you spoken to him?" I inquired.

"Yes, we went to talk to their family today. Everything seems okay, and we will discuss it further," he reported.

"That's good news, Manoj," I said.

In truth, I was well aware of this boy and felt joy for my daughter, albeit tinged with a hint of unease. I couldn't pinpoint the source of my disquiet.

"They have visited the boy's family and are satisfied with this association," I told Laxmi one night.

"Yes, I know. Babli informed me. This is really pleasant news we have heard after a long time," Laxmi remarked.

"Yes, God bless the children," I added.

However, I couldn't express to Laxmi why I was upset.

In life, 2 things bring both joy and pain: expectation and acceptance. Expectations, when unfulfilled, breed pain, while acceptance brings relief. Yet, I found myself wrestling with expectations. Maybe my expectations weren't entirely unjustified.

Since Shalu's marriage discussions, I had involved Manoj from day one. He was present during meetings with potential families, engagements, and various ceremonies. He played a pivotal role in these significant moments. Similarly, for Vicky's wedding, Manoj was there every step of the way. I even included his and Babli's names in the invitation cards, acknowledging their importance in my children's lives. Were my expectations too high?

Perhaps there was a reason, a beginning. He would include me in future occasions. Or maybe I was overthinking. Prerna was no less than a daughter to me, and I also wanted to meet the family and the boy to ensure everything was in order. Sleep eluded me the entire night.

"We are going for Ankit's Roka today," Manoj informed us one day. "We're going to their home – Babli, Poonam, her husband, and myself. It's not a big function," he mentioned.

"Congratulations, Manoj. Wish you all the best," I conveyed.

"Thank-you, Jijaji."

Believe me, I am not usually this restless, but an inexplicable unease had taken hold of me. Throughout the day, I felt joy for Prerna but a lingering discomfort within myself. Was I expecting too much?

"Congratulations, the date has been fixed for February, but the engagement will be after a month," Manoj shared over the phone.

"That's great news, Manoj," I responded.

"Yes, we will book a place for the engagement soon. They've entrusted me with this responsibility," he informed.

"Of course, Manoj. Please let me know if I can be of any help," I offered.

"Yes, I will."

The wheels of life continued to turn, each moment pregnant with a tapestry of emotions, a weave of joy and discomfort, expectations and acceptance.

"We have booked Radisson Blu in Vaishali for the engagement," Manoj shared one day.

"That's great. What's the programme?" I asked.

"I will come and discuss it with you," he replied.

"OK."

They arrived with a sweet box, initiating discussions on various wedding details. The atmosphere was filled with happiness as preparations for the D-day were in full swing. I assured myself that I would meet the boy and his family during the engagement, and a sense of contentment settled within me.

"Come to Noida tomorrow. We'll proceed to the venue together," Manoj instructed me a day before.

"Sure, we'll be there."

Preparations for the engagement were underway, and gifts and other essentials were sent to the venue in advance. A makeup artist was summoned to the hotel to prepare Prerna for the grand occasion. Excitement pervaded every corner.

We reached the venue on time. Panditji performed the necessary rituals on the stage, and after the pooja, preparations for the ring ceremony began. The party ensued, with everyone revelling in the joyous occasion. I eagerly awaited the moment to meet the boy and his family.

As the night progressed, rituals were completed, and it was time to bid farewell to the guests. I waited anxiously for an introduction, but none came. My disappointment was palpable. Had my expectations been too much?

Observing my distressed expression, Laxmi sensed my disappointment and sent Vicky to inquire.

"What happened, papa?" he asked.

"Nothing, why are you asking?" I replied.

"Put your hand on my head and tell me. You look very upset," he insisted, gently guiding my hand to his head.

Tears welled up in my eyes as I poured out my feelings to him, urging him not to share this with anyone.

Unable to resist, Vicky confided in Shalu, who, in turn, informed Babli.

"Jijaji, please come," Manoj called me.

"Meet Mr. Saluja; he is Ankit's father, and he is my elder brother and brother-in-law," he introduced.

We exchanged pleasantries and engaged in some formal conversation. Unable to bear the discomfort any longer, I asked Laxmi to leave with me. The children stayed behind for their own celebration.

We travelled in silence.

"Please come home for lunch today," Manoj phoned me the next day.

"Sorry, Manoj, I have to go to the office," I said.

"No way. Whether you take leave or anything, you have to come," he insisted.

"OK," I agreed.

Attempting to downplay the situation, I convinced myself not to make a fuss and keep quiet. However, drama unfolded in Noida. Babli relentlessly pursued Manoj for what she perceived as an insult to us by not introducing us to the in-laws.

We joined them for lunch but returned home still feeling upset. Unable to contain my emotions, I sat with my laptop and penned down my thoughts to find relief:

"Dear Manoj,

I don't know where to start. We have travelled the journey of life together for a long time, and looking back, it's still vivid. Over time, negative thoughts have been accumulating, but being a positive person, I always brushed them aside. However, the fact remains, and ignoring it won't change it. These thoughts bring a sense of pain.

I vividly recall our first meeting over 30 years ago. You were an innocent boy with love, respect, and affection in your eyes. We evolved from friends to good friends and best friends, reaching a level of brotherhood or real brothers—only God knows. This became possible due to your companionship, responsibility, and the stress-free environment you provided during our life's journey. I profoundly thank God for sending one of His choicest human beings to bring satisfaction to me in all times—good or bad.

If I start listing your good qualities, I could write pages, describing each detail, but I won't. The way you took care of Mataji when she was terribly ill, your support when Laxmi fell ill, and your unwavering presence when I needed someone—all these instances stand out. The responsibility you shouldered for Shalu's marriage, your support during my illness, and your involvement in Vicky's wedding are just a few examples. I never missed my brother because you were there for me.

We never differentiated between our children; you know that. After Vicky's marriage, we eagerly awaited Abhishek or Prerna's marriage. When I heard about Prerna's engagement, it brought immense joy, though accompanied by the natural anxiety of sending our daughter into an unknown home. It was only natural to want to meet, talk to, and understand them. Was it wrong? I don't think so.

I understood your limitations, anxiously awaiting the D-day. I won't describe everything here. Whatever happened on that day, I'm still working on getting over it all. It's going to hurt for a while, and I'm afraid to let my feelings out. It was your decision, and you're always right. Please don't ever think I am blaming you. If there's anyone to blame, it's me for dreaming so big. I'm reminding myself of my limits and my level. In every relationship, the person who keeps the other ahead leads the relationship, even if it may seem otherwise. Keeping the other person ahead means saying yes to them, even when you don't agree. This is what I did in every happening in my life. I need time to get over the shock, hurt, anger, sadness, and confusion. I will most probably have these feelings repeat themselves for some time, and that's okay. It's my mind and heart, and I can be in charge of how long it will take to move on. I will try not to dwell for too long and miss out on the great things that life has to offer. Sorrows are always because of expectations, and when you don't expect anything, they disappear. Now, I am counselling myself not to be disappointed when nobody stands with me. I am thankful to those who left me because they taught me, I can do it alone. Once upon a time, I used to think that whatever I am doing is the best, but under these circumstances, I am trying to change myself. In fact, I have changed a lot.

Days slip into weeks, weeks turn into months, and months transform into years. Calendars are changing, and so am I.

Yes, I am changing. In certain things, age has mellowed me down, in others, I have become more aggressive. Sometimes I find myself acting wise, and sometimes I just go crazy. Certain issues will have me speaking vociferously, whereas at others, I just shrug and remain silent.

Yes, I am changing. I no longer bargain with poor vegetable and fruit vendors. After all, a few rupees more won't burn a hole in my pocket, but it might help the poor fellow save for his daughter's school fees.

Yes, I am changing. I have learned not to correct people even when I know they are wrong. The onus of making everyone perfect is not on me. Peace is more precious than perfection.

Yes, I am changing. I give compliments freely and generously. After all, it's a mood enhancer not only for the recipient but also for me.

Yes, I am changing. I am learning not to let others make me feel incompetent. I might not be good at certain things, but I am excellent at others.

Yes, I am changing. I walk away from people who don't value me. After all, they might not know my worth, but I do.

Yes, I am changing. I remain cool when someone plays dirty politics to outrun me in the rat race. After all, I am not a rat, and neither am I in any race.

Yes, I am changing. I am learning not to be embarrassed by my emotions. After all, it's my emotions that make me human.

Yes, I am changing. I now tell people if I like them. After all, there is nothing wrong with liking someone.

Yes, I am changing. I have learned that it's better to drop the ego than to break a relationship. After all, my ego will keep me aloof whereas with relationships I will never be alone.

Yes, I am changing. I have learned to live each day as if it were the last. After all, it might be the last.

Yes, I am changing. I am doing what makes me happy. After all, I am responsible for my happiness, and I owe it to myself. And I am loving the new me!

There is no ill feeling now. Please rest assured; you will never feel embarrassed because of me at least. I will definitely try to be normal whenever I attend the functions. Of course, I will have to attend all the functions and enjoy because they are my own children.

Vinod."

After penning this letter, I refrained from sending it to Manoj or anyone else. It served as a cathartic exercise, a means to release the stress that had gripped me.

As time passed, the turbulence within me settled. I pushed the incident to the recesses of my mind, immersing myself in the demands of daily work. The relentless ticking of the clock ushered in the day of the wedding, and we found ourselves brimming with both excitement and anxiety. The chosen venue for this grand celebration was the opulent Country Inn.

"Papa, mummy, you have to go to Singapore for your wedding anniversary," Vicky announced a day before the wedding.

"Are we going on the 24th, the anniversary date?" I queried with surprise.

"No, you have to go on the 22nd because you're celebrating your anniversary on a cruise," he revealed.

"But Prerna's wedding is on the 17th. How can we leave so early?" Laxmi questioned.

"We've made all the arrangements. Priyanka will finish the packing before the wedding," Vicky assured.

"Why are you spending so much?" Laxmi probed. "How much do you have to pay?"

"One crore. Why are you asking so many questions? You're going to Singapore, mummy, just enjoy!" Vicky responded.

"Okay, but if you could come along, it would be more fun," I suggested.

"You enjoy your day," he insisted.

"Thank-you, children!! God bless you."

Amid the whirlwind of wedding rituals, Prerna approached me.

"Masad, you have to come to our bachelor's party for sure," she declared, exercising her right as my niece.

"What will I do in your youngsters' group, Prerna?" I questioned.

"No, you are still young, and you are coming. It's an order," she asserted.

"Okay, I will come."

"This is like my Masad," she exclaimed, radiating joy.

The bachelor's party unfolded in the basement of Noida, a worry-free zone as our children were safely ensconced at home.

"Meet my Masad, Ankit. I call him Masad, but he is no less than my own father," Prerna introduced me to her fiancé.

"Namaste Masad. I've heard so much about you from Prerna," Ankit greeted.

"Prerna talks too much. I am just nothing, Ankit," I humbly replied.

Laughter echoed as our conversation unfolded. The atmosphere lightened.

"Listen, we have to go for Mata ki Chowki today, remember?" Laxmi reminded me.

"Yes, I remember. I will come on time," I assured.

"Not on time, but you have to take leave today," she directed.

"Okay, I will talk to my team and then take leave," I agreed.

"I am on leave today," I informed her.

"That's good. Let's go purchase some gifts for today," she suggested.

Reflecting on the journey from Prerna's birth until this moment, I decided to pen letters—one for Ankit and another for Prerna. Some thoughts flow more authentically from the heart than the mind. The letters were transformed into hard copies, framed, and ready to be presented. The letters read:

Dear Little and Beloved Girl,

It's a mixed feeling - happiness and sadness both. Sometimes I imagined how I would feel on that day. It is a great feeling that fills my heart. I wish you much happiness in your future home and that you 2 may always be united. You will unite your life with the man who won your heart; you are all grown up now but remember I will always be there for my little princess whenever you require my help. I feel as if you had recently come into our lives; now you are leaving with your husband because that is how life is, but you will always be my princess. I wish you happiness and prosperity in your home. The dream of every father is to see their children move ahead with their lives; that is why I am so happy today, as my daughter will join the love of her life to be companions forever. As far as emotions of love for another person are concerned, I think it is coming from inside and no doctor can inject the same. But in your case, I hope you people understood each and everything, as you are very intelligent and give and take 100% after marriage. I do not require any promise for this but hope for the best because I want everything for you.

We are happy for your wedding life but sad because you will not be with us, and there is a vacuum in life after 17th Feb. Today when I look back, I cannot even imagine that you were not with your Mausi and Mausaji as their own daughter since your childhood. We always feel with satisfaction that you have been with us since your birth. Even your mausi must be feeling the same thing, but because of her nature, she could not tell this to you. I will never forget the way you introduced us to Ankit. We both were thrilled when you told him that you are not related to us by blood, but in a real sense, we are your parents. It's a great compliment.

For a daughter, her father is a hero and her best friend. She always looks up to him for advice, for support, for motivation, and for teaching the valuable lessons of life. Right from birth until the later days of life, a father and a daughter always share a special bond filled with love, trust and emotions. And marriage is one such happy and exciting occasion where every daughter wants some guidance from her father that can help her in the new life. There are a few things that a girl is probably already aware of but hearing it from father will make a lot of difference to her. Most Indian fathers love to leave things unspoken but we are more friends than father-daughter.

The happiest day in a girl's life is when she becomes a bride and marries the man of her dreams in the blissful presence of her family, friends and relatives. But vidaai comes as a paradox when the bride cries on her most awaited day.

Every girl knows that she has to leave her family behind one day and embrace the family of her husband. But when the moment actually comes when she is literally leaving behind her family, a bride gets overwhelmed with emotions. There are a number of emotions and feelings that a bride goes through during her vidaai.

Till the day she gets married, her mother is the backbone of her life. She could rely on her for each and everything. She knows that her mother would be by her side whenever she got unwell, or when she could not get good marks in the exam. How can she stay away from her ever-understanding mother who never asked to be understood by her in return? Now, as she leaves her mother's side and herself takes those responsibilities in her new family, she is not sure who will pamper her in the same way in her new family?

Till yesterday, you were daddy's little girl and now suddenly, you are grown up to take responsibility for a new family. Your father went on to any extent to bring a smile on your face. You know that he left no stone unturned to fulfil your wishes and give the best to his daughter. The one, who taught you to walk and also to be independent in life, is now letting you go away from him. You must be sceptical, if anyone would ever share that special place in your heart where your father lives?

You surely had never-ending fights with brother/sister over the slightest of reasons. But your siblings acted more like a best friend whenever you needed them. Those moments might have been annoying back then, but now they are priceless to cherish for life. How can you forget growing up together, sharing the same toys, clothes, chocolates, and literally sharing your life with them? Now as you leave them behind, that feeling of parting from a best friend fills your eyes with tears.

You have special stories at every nook and corner of the house. How can you ever forget the place where you grew up? This is the place where you spent almost a quarter of your life, and now you will come here as a visitor. Your room, which you decorated with great passion or your favourite chair on the dining table where you always sat for your dinner - you will miss all those little things of your house. The memories of the place that you called your home might soon fade out. And you will call another home as your own.

When daughters are small, they see in their dad an exemplary man and role model, and fathers look at their daughters and see in them their little princesses. When the day of the marriage arrives, many feelings converge in the mind and heart of the father.

When you don't know if you should cry or laugh, but the tears come anyway. Looking at the 2 men you love the most leaves you overwhelmed.

Always remember, your Masad and Mausi are always there for you.

With lots of Love,

Mausi & Masad

The letters served as a testament to the profound emotions swirling within me as my niece, Prerna, embarked on this new chapter of her life.

The letter to Ankit unfolded with the weight of a father's emotions, delicately etched on the canvas of love and concern:

"Dear Ankit,

I had contemplated starting this letter by addressing you as the 'new' family of our daughter, but it seems inappropriate. Now that she is stepping into the sacred bond of marriage, you are 'the family' for her. We don't harbour any reservations about that; in fact, we wish for our daughter to prioritise 'you' in her life now. It's time for us to take a backseat, and we willingly accept it, but with a humble request—please keep her happy!

We are more than confident that after meeting you on the 27th of January, she will find happiness with you that perhaps exceeds what she experienced here. Yet, like all parents, we are preoccupied with our daughter's joy. Hence, I find myself repeating this earnest plea—please keep her happy!

She has never been, and will never be, a burden to us. She is the reason why we breathe and smile. This marriage is an inevitable part of the natural order, and, bound by our culture, we are sending her to your home. She was the sunshine of our dwelling, and now, she will illuminate yours. Entrusting our world to you, we implore you to ensure it remains beautiful. We are handing over our princess; please make sure she remains a queen. We raised her with our sweat and blood, and now, she is wonderfully perfect. For all the care, love, beauty, and warmth she brings into your lives, all we ask for is her happiness— please keep her happy!

If, at times, you feel our daughter has said or done something wrong, feel free to counsel her, but handle her with love. She is delicate. If, at times, she feels low, be with her; she just needs a little of your attention. If, at times, she feels unwell, show her care; it's the best medicine for her. If, at times, she falls short of a responsibility, feel free to discipline her, but sympathise with her—she is still learning. Please understand her—please keep her happy!

We don't mind not seeing her for months. We don't mind not talking to her daily. We would be more than happy if she doesn't remember us much. Our only life's purpose has been our daughter's happiness, now in your hands. I beg you, please keep her happy!

Dear son-in-law, these words may not mean much now, but if you are blessed with a daughter someday, you will understand them better. You will find every beat of your heart echoing—please keep her happy!

When a girl gets married, she steps out of her own Heaven into a world full of uncertainties just to keep a family running and lives blooming—please keep her happy!

Only parents can truly understand what it is to give a daughter away. The little doll they cherished since birth has grown so fast, leaving them with a heartache. Although they always knew she was destined to leave, they secretly believed there was more time. Wasn't it just yesterday that she played with the neighbourhood children in little pigtails? Time sneaked up on them, and now, they find themselves watching her leave. It's painful; it rips at your heart to know you're returning to an empty house, leaving a part of your heart behind. I beg once more—please keep her happy!

They go through the joy mixed with pain that every parent of the bride experiences. They are parents like any other, cherishing a daughter since birth. They think about her departure and the bittersweet emotions they endure as their pride and joy leaves them. They cry, and their siblings are the only ones who truly understand. Their little doll has transformed into a beautiful woman. She leaves her home to brighten someone else's, leaving behind the shadow of her absence. I request you—please keep her happy!

Trying to be encouraging, they tell her she was just a treasure belonging to someone else; they were merely caretakers. All they wish now is for her eternal happiness. They pray to God for her well-being and good health. They tell their daughter to be happy as she's found her prince charming. Bidding her adieu, they cry their hearts out, torn between wanting to let her go and holding on to her forever. Silent tears course down their cheeks by the end of the ceremony.

With folded hands—please keep her happy!

With lots of love,

Mausi & Mausaji"

As Prerna embarked on her new journey, we bid her farewell with moist eyes, a blend of joy and sorrow intertwining in the tapestry of our emotions.

The return from the wedding marked the beginning of another adventure—our first foreign trip to Singapore. The excitement and anxiety filled the air as Priyanka confirmed the completion of our packing.

"Looks alright, but I need to remember if we've forgotten anything," Laxmi exclaimed with anticipation. This was a momentous occasion, and the credit belonged to our beloved children.

"Please keep in touch through WhatsApp," Vicky advised.

"Don't worry, we'll talk to you upon reaching there," I assured.

"I've made all the arrangements, booked a package. A car will receive you upon your arrival, and all bookings are sorted," Vicky explained.

"I've kept some Singapore currency with mummy. Don't be miser; spend as you wish," he continued.

"I know. With these arrangements, there's no need to worry," I replied.

The foreign land awaited us, and as our plane touched down, the bustling atmosphere greeted us. The anticipation of being in an unfamiliar place heightened our senses.

"How will we recognise the person who comes to receive us?" Laxmi questioned.

"Don't worry; they'll have a placard," I reassured.

Seated at the airport, we waited eagerly for our escort.

"Are you Vinod Sharma?" a voice inquired.

"Yes, have you come to receive us?" I responded.

"Yes, please come with me. I'll take you to the hotel, Boss. In 2 hours, someone will come to take you for sightseeing," he informed.

"OK."

The hotel, a pristine and well-maintained haven, greeted us. Excitement bubbled within us as we freshened up, ready to explore the enchanting city.

"This is the reception. Someone will take you down; please come," the voice on the phone informed.

"Yes, we are coming," I replied.

A bus, carrying a mix of Indian and foreign passengers, ushered us through various places.

"It's amazing!" Laxmi exclaimed.

"Yes, please enjoy," I urged, capturing the moments with photographs.

The following day led us to a place with electric tricycle games.

"I won't sit on this. I might slip and fall," Laxmi expressed her fear.

"Don't worry; I'll be behind you. If anything happens, I'll take care," I assured.

"OK, if you insist, I will try," she agreed.

Even I was nervous. What would happen in this foreign land if she got hurt?

"Come ahead; I'm enjoying it," she laughed. I stared at her face, witnessing her engage in childlike activities after a long time, feeling a sense of satisfaction.

"Today, we're going on a cruise for 3 nights. Pack up and come down," someone informed us on the phone.

"OK, we are coming!" I exclaimed, sharing Laxmi's enthusiasm.

"Everything feels like a dream," Laxmi rejoiced.

"Yes, all thanks to our extraordinary children," I agreed.

Memorable moments unfolded as we sailed on the cruise. Our room, with a balcony overlooking the vast sea, provided a breathtaking view. Laxmi, fearful of water, refrained from sitting there.

Every corner echoed with joy—music, games, and more.

The day to return arrived, bringing with it a mix of excitement and a longing to share our experiences with our children. This journey had not only marked a foreign exploration but had also etched moments of joy and togetherness in the album of our lives.

The familiar embrace of home welcomed us as Priyanka and Vicky, the epitomes of filial love, stood at the airport to receive us. In the comfort of our homeland, we settled into the car, and Vicky, with eager anticipation, inquired about our journey.

"How was the trip?" he asked.

"It was wonderful and amazing," Laxmi exclaimed in a cheerful voice, reminiscent of a child enthralled by a newfound joy.

"Now you will have no regret that you could not celebrate your 25th anniversary," Vicky remarked.

"Yes, there is no regret in anything in life. We have children like you who take care of their parents so much," I responded.

Overwhelmed by what our children had done for us, Laxmi and I found ourselves basking in the warmth of their love.

"We have to give something to them also," Laxmi mentioned one day.

"They have everything. What can we give?" I asked.

"I don't know, but we have to give them something exclusive that keeps them happy," Laxmi asserted.

"I can write a thank-you letter to them; that's something I can do," I suggested.

"Then what are you waiting for?" Laxmi encouraged.

Seated with pen and paper, I began to write:

"Dear Shalu, Vicky, and Priyanka,

We find ourselves feeling immensely relaxed today. Not just because our recent foreign sojourn revitalised us, but due to the initial success in a mission I had been working on secretly for quite some time. The time has come to unveil it to you.

Throughout my life, I observed that we often remain ignorant of our feelings toward our near and dear ones, failing to express our love and care for them, though it resides deep within our hearts. We repeatedly read stories about conveying thanks and apologies to strangers. When we wish to address them, we politely say 'Excuse me.' However, when it comes to our family, we tend to take their love for granted, assuming it is their duty to care for us. Rarely do we express our love with 3 simple words—'I love you'—to our spouse, siblings, or parents. I think never. We may utter these magical words only when they are critically ill, far away, or missed intensely. Even then, we hesitate to convey them verbally.

I felt this void many times in my life but failed to express it, either verbally or in writing. The first time was during Shalu's farewell, where her absence was palpable, but I shied away from expressing my emotions. The second instance was when your mother was hospitalised in 2001. I cried out loud for the first time in my life, praying fervently for her return. Yet, I couldn't convey these sentiments directly to her. It was only in 2010, on her birthday, that I mustered the courage to express my feelings in a letter. Shalu narrated it to her, and the room was filled with tears. That moment made me realise the impact of verbalising our emotions to our family.

Since then, I made it a practice to write on every occasion for our family members, and the responses were heartwarming. Although I conveyed my feelings, there was a desire to inspire others to follow the same path.

This mission can be deemed an initial success because I not only receive detailed replies but also heartfelt letters on my birthday and anniversary. God bless you all and keep up the tradition. Expressing ourselves requires thought, and in that process, both positive and negative aspects enter our minds. We should always appreciate the good and apologise for the bitter experiences. I hope this contagion of expressing feelings spreads throughout the world. Once that happens, we may never hear of depression again. Although we might not witness this transformation, our souls will undoubtedly rejoice.

Now, turning to our Singapore trip—it was so relaxing and comfortable that it felt like we lived an entirely new life in just one week. Allow us to extend our sincere thanks to all of you. Not only was it a rejuvenating experience, but it also instilled confidence in us that we can manage independently. Over time, you all provided us with so much comfort that we became dependent on you for even the smallest things. Thank-you for reviving our confidence in being independent during this trip.

Expressing our gratitude is not a mere formality; it is a deep and significant feeling.

Thank-you, each one of you, for being there for us. Thank-you for overlooking our faults and consistently encouraging us.

Throughout my life, I've known that I am a rich man because I have you. Thank-you for everything you've done for us, my dear and lovely family.

For your understanding, sometimes beyond your strength; for your invaluable help, please accept our best thanks.

For your patience and kindness, for your invaluable advice and devotion, please accept our deep appreciation.

Your love and understanding are the sources of our strength. Please accept our heartfelt thanks for that.

Friendship is said to be the most valuable thing in the world. So, accept our grateful appreciation for being that valuable to us.

Accept our heartfelt thanks, dear family, for your allegiance and devotion.

For all these years of moral support and unswerving loyalty, accept our thanks and gratitude, my dear family.

This thank-you note is sent to express how much we appreciate your thoughtfulness.

The gift of family is incomparable. You all are the source of our strength and sustenance—thank-you for your devotion and moral support.

Words often prove inadequate to express our joy on the trip. You made us so comfortable that we never felt like we were in another country.

We are what we are because you stood by us when the world turned its back on us. A million thank-yous for your care.

We are really glad that we're family. Thanking God for having you in our lives.

Yours,

Mummy & Papa"

As we returned to the comforting routine of our lives, one day, Vicky approached us with a solemn expression.

"Papa, mummy, I want to talk to you," he said.

"Yes," I responded.

"I am getting a promotion in the company," he announced.

"That's great news, but why do you look sad?" I inquired.

"I will have to get transferred to Hyderabad," he revealed.

"It's alright. When will you go?" I asked nonchalantly.

"It's not a joke, papa. If I go, you and mummy will have to accompany us," he stated.

"How can that be possible, Vicky? I am running my own business, and mummy can't adjust so quickly with everyone," I explained.

"Yes, Vicky, please don't miss this opportunity. We will visit you like we used to visit Jaipur," Laxmi suggested.

"No, mummy, either I refuse the promotion, or you will go with me," he asserted.

"Okay, we will think about it," Laxmi replied.

"Have you talked to Shalu?" I asked.

"Yes, she is also reluctant," he confirmed.

"Let's consider it. How much time do you have to decide?" I inquired.

"I have to inform them of my decision by next week," he stated.

"Okay, we will think, but I believe you should not refuse," I concluded.

We discussed this with Shalu, who was hesitant. Deepak, too, was not agreeable to this proposition.

Ultimately, Vicky refused the promotion. It surprised everyone that Vicky turned down a career opportunity for the sake of his parents. In an era where children seldom consider their parents when it comes to their careers, we felt a sense of pride. Our children were indeed exceptional.

"Think again, Vicky. Such opportunities are rare in life," I suggested.

"No, papa, life doesn't end here. I will get another chance in this organisation when the right time comes," he affirmed.

"Papa, we have to discuss something with you," Vicky spoke to me over the phone one day.

"Yes, please tell," I replied.

"You know, this is mummy's 60th birthday, and we want to celebrate it in a grand way," he said.

"Yes, I'd like that too, but let's be mindful of the finances," I suggested.

"Don't worry about that. I've already talked to didi, and we'll share the expenses," he assured me.

"I also want to contribute. Please let me know," I insisted.

"No, papa, we will handle it."

"What about the venue? Where will it be?" I inquired.

"We've spoken to the Country Inn Hotel. They will charge a reasonable price," he informed.

"What if I also contribute?" I persisted.

"No, papa, don't worry. Your children are capable enough to handle things," he reassured.

"Who all will be coming to the party?" I asked.

"Mama's family, Babli didi's family, didi's family, and our family. That's all," he replied.

"It will be around 25-30 people. It will be costly," I expressed my concern.

"Don't worry. After all, it's her 60th birthday. She will be very happy," he said.

"You're right. She says no, but she is very fond of such parties," I acknowledged.

"Yes, papa. That's why we decided to do this."

The more I reflect, the stronger my faith in God becomes. It is true that God doesn't grant us the choice to choose our relatives, which is why we must accept our parents, siblings, and relatives as they are. However, He has bestowed upon us the choice to pick our life partners and the in-laws of our children. Is it an easy choice? I doubt it. Couples are said to be made in Heaven, and pearls and the most valued diamonds are not destined for everyone. God has adorned our lives with the choicest pearls from His treasure. First, Laxmi came into our lives, transforming our house into a home. Now, as the time comes to choose life partners for our children, I feel incredibly fortunate to have Deepak and Priyanka in our lives. I bow my head in gratitude to God for blessing us with individuals like them.

The depth of the ocean may be measurable if given a try, but the depth of our love for each other is immeasurable. This is why God has created numerous distractions, for the depth of love and affection from our children and their spouses cannot be quantified. Whenever we need them, they are present, whether we call them or not.

"Mummy, what do you want on your birthday?" Priyanka and Vicky sat beside her one day.

"I have everything, and moreover, my children are so caring that there is no desire now," she said.

"Thanks, mummy, but if you tell us, we will bring a gift of your choice; otherwise, we will bring what we think is best," Vicky said.

"Are you ready?" I asked Laxmi on her special day.

"Yes, give me 5 minutes."

"Hurry up, everyone must have reached the hotel," I said.

"OK, coming."

"Hi Shalu, how are you?" Shalu and Deepak were standing there when we arrived.

"I am fine. Why are you so late?" Shalu said.

"The birthday girl was getting ready," and everybody laughed.

Within half an hour, everyone had arrived at the lovely party venue.

"Let's cut the cake," I announced.

"Yes, please come, everybody," Vicky said.

There was a glow on Laxmi's face like never before.

"Happy birthday to you…," we sang a song for her.

"Where is your gift?" Laxmi whispered in my ear.

"You will get it very soon," I replied.

Ladies and gentlemen, today I have written something for my beloved wife, and that's my gift to her.

"Leave it, Jijaji. We can't understand what you wrote in English," Babli exclaimed.

"That's the best part. You and your sister will also understand it today because I have had it translated into Hindi," I said.

"That's great. What's the delay now?"

"OK, here is the letter which Vicky will read," I announced.

"प्रिय पत्नी जीवनसंगिनी,

जिंदगी एक किताब है और हर गुजरता साल उस किताब के पन्ने। पन्ने उन सुनहरी यादों के जो हमने एक साथ संजोए। पन्ने उन सारे पलों के जो हमने एक दूसरे का हाथ पकड़ के साथ में जिए। पन्ने उन मीठी नोकझोंक के, रूठने के मनाने के, मान के मनुहार के। पन्ने हर इन सांसों के जो मैंने तुम्हारे नाम पर ली और तुमने मेरे नाम पर।

आज जब तुम अपनी जिंदगी के साठवें बसंत में प्रवेश कर रही हो। मैं खुशी से डबडबाई आंखों से - हाथों में वरमाला थामे शर्माती सकुचाती 18 साल की लक्ष्मी को देख रहा हूं। जो आज भी मन से 18 साल की ही है और मेरे हाथ थामे 42 कदम चलकर उन्हीं नजरों से मुझे देख रही है जैसे उसने हमारी पहली मुलाकात में मुझे देखा था।

42 साल 42 कदम।

हम मिले, हमारा एक छोटा सा घरौंदा बना। पता ही नहीं चला कि कब हम एक दूसरे के प्यार में इतना खो गए कि हम मां बाप की अवस्था को पार करके नाना नानी बाबा दादी की अवस्था में आ गए और आज जब यादों के पन्ने पलट रहा हूं तो दिल से दुआ निकल रही है कि ये सफर यूं ही चलता रहे और हम एक दूसरे को हाथ थामे बस चलते रहें।

शादी में सात फेरे होते हैं - सात वचन दिए जाते हैं - सात जन्मों का साथ है - इंद्रधनुष में भी सात रंग होते है - एक सप्ताह में भी सात दिन होते हैं - कुछ तो है सात में - साथ में - सांस में - अरदास में - अहसास में।

जिंदगी करबटें बदलती रही। धूप छांव भी आते जाते रहे। कोई भी सफर सुहाना नहीं होता। लेकिन तुम्हारे साथ सफर का पता ही नहीं चला। बस लगा कि मैं अपनी दुल्हन के साथ अभी भी अग्नि के सात फेरे ही ले रहा हूं। जब कभी जिंदगी सुनसान हुई और मैंने तुम्हारे साथ चाय की चुस्कियां लगाकर बातें करी लगा कि ईश्वर को साक्षी मानकर सात वचन ही पढ़ रहा हूं। जब जिंदगी बेरंग हुई तो तुमने उनमें इंद्रधनुष के सातों रंग भर दिए। सच में सात में कुछ तो बात है - साथ में कुछ तो बात है

लोग भगवान के मंदिर कुछ ना कुछ मांगने जाते हैं और मैं जाता हूं उनका दिल से शुक्रिया अदा करने। मांगना क्या जब मुझे बिन मांगे ही इतना कुछ मिल गया। तुम आई तो मेरा घर बना। मेरे माता पिता को तुमने अपने माता पिता से भी बढ़कर मान सम्मान और देखभाल दी। कभी कहीं बहुत अच्छा किया होगा मैंने जो तुमने मुझे इतना प्यार करने वाले बच्चे दिए। तिनका तिनका जोड़ा और मुझ गरीब को दुनिया का सबसे अमीर इंसान बना दिया। और मेरे जैसा अमीर आदमी भगवान के दर पर मांगने नहीं शुक्रिया अदा करने ही जा सकता है।

प्रकृति ने हम सारे जीव, जंतुओं, पौधों, पक्षियों, हर जीवित चीज को - चाहे वह बोल सकती हो या ना बोल सकती हो - एक चीज जरूर बख्शी है - कम्युनिकेशन - हम जब दुखी होते हैं तो मुरझा जाते हैं। खुश होते हैं तो खिलखिला जाते हैं और जिनको हम प्यार करते हैं उनको सिर्फ छू कर यह एहसास दिला देते हैं कि हम उनको कितना प्यार करते हैं। और यह अनकहे शब्द पूरी जिंदगी की कहानी बयां कर देते हैं।

शायद जिंदगी की आपाधापी में मैं कम मौकों पर ही यह कह पाया तो मैं तुम्हें कितना चाहता हूं। लेकिन आज जब हमारा प्यार 42वां बसंत देख रहा है तो मैं छत में जाकर चिल्ला चिल्ला कर दुनिया को बताना चाहता हूं कि मैं तुम्हें कितना प्यार करता हूं।

आज जब ईश्वर ने हमें इतना कुछ दिया फिर भी हम सब एक चीज बार-बार मांगते रहते हैं - वह है तुम्हारी एक मासूम सी मुस्कान। जिसे कमाने के लिए मैं और हमारे बच्चे आज भी जी जान लगा देते हैं। आज तुम्हारे जन्मदिन पर हम तुम्हें गिफ्ट में अपना सारा प्यार, सम्मान और अपनापन सौंपते हैं और रिटर्न गिफ्ट में बस वही मासूम सी मुस्कान चाहते हैं और हमें जानते हैं कि तुम हमें कभी निराश नहीं करोगी।

Happy birthday to you my best friend, best companion, my wife, my lover.

शब्द कम पड़ जाते हैं - यह एहसास दिलाने को तुम मुझे कितनी प्रिय हो । बस मेरा हाथ थामे रहना । मेरी गलतियों को माफ करती रहना और यूं ही मुस्कुराती रहना । I LOVE YOU VERY MUCH"

Here is the English version: -

"My dear life partner,

The thought of turning 60 might make you feel old. Whether you feel young or old is really up to you. Although it's your 60th birthday, it is nowhere written to feel old. On the other hand, please remember 42 years of our togetherness. It's a milestone at which rare people reach. Take it nice and easy. It's your special 60. However, for me you are always a young lady whom I love the most in this world and get inspiration for many things like strong will to name a few. You will see 100 without a doubt – Aamin!!!!!

I don't know if my love for my wife is important in the whole world. But I know that my life is richer and happier and less lonely and more joyful because of you. And I know the world needs love because it makes life worth living. Meeting you long ago rendered the inevitable loneliness of life more than tolerable, it rendered life meaningful. What began as a glance has lasted a lifetime. I was blessed.

A birthday is very important to a child. The cake, the candles and gifts are something which they look forward to weeks on end. As we get older, we begin to realise that more important than materialistic things are the things we celebrate for those who are the closest to us.

Thank-you for making me a father to these beautiful children standing in front of me, I am blessed to have the opportunity to raise these amazing children of mine and have never been prouder.

For all who are lucky enough to know you, understand that you are one who would do more for others than yourself. A quality which I am sure we all agree is very rare these days. You always look to see the positive in life, no matter how dark and gloomy things may be, something which you have allowed for me to adopt which has changed my life dramatically for the better.

The more you attain age, the more valuable you become. In my opinion, your value is priceless. I am happy that your inner child is still ageless. It is true that sometimes there are some sweet and sour moments between us like not agreeing on certain issues, but it is also true that I always surrender, and this is the reason we walked so long together and are still fond of each other. But one thing is same from the inception of our introduction till date is that you are still very shy of telling something you wish or in your mind to your own children and me. However, over a period of time, we understand what you require by your one smile only.

It seems that everyone knows that you turned a year older except me. In my eyes, you are exactly the way that you were when I met you for the first time – stunning and gorgeous even after becoming a grandmother. As you blow the candles on your birthday cake, I want to tell you what a wonderful wife you make. Without you in my life, my heart would have bled. With you, I look forward to a wonderful life ahead. I know you have a lot of things to do, so I am taking them off your hands and doing them for you. The tea seems tastier and satisfying when I make it for you in the morning. Very few people meet their soul mates, but I have been fortunate enough to marry this special someone.

Every now and then someone comes into your life, and they turn it upside down in a good way, and you are that someone for me. You are my life and I wish you a very happy birthday. To my beautiful wife, I hope this year brings you as much joy and happiness that you have brought and continue to bring into our life. I wake up every morning and thank the Lord for bringing you into my life. With each year, I will love you more. Remember that your best years are still ahead of you, and I will be there for you at life's every up and down and in-between. Let's make this a birthday to remember. It's all about you today and I want to make you feel like the happiest woman alive.

I don't feel embarrassed in telling all my friends that you are in charge of my life. I feel lucky and proud to have a woman as hardworking and focused as you are my wife. Your birthday is the perfect opportunity to say SORRY for all the fights and arguments, THANK-YOU for all the sacrifices you've made, and I LOVE YOU for everything that you mean to me. I feel so blessed to have such a beautiful and supportive life partner like you. I wish you true happiness on your birthday, and always. No words can express my feelings for you. You are my love, my sunshine, my life. More than a wife in you I have found a friend for life.

On birthdays people wish so many things, but for me there are just 2 words – Always and Never. Always be by my side and never leave me. Best birthday wishes to the perfect woman in the world who chose to love an imperfect man like me. My goal is to keep a smile on your face. And when it starts to fade, I will do whatever it takes to brighten your day. As we grow old together, we will change. But one thing will stay the same and that is our love, the glue that holds us together. Your birthday cake is symbolic of how your sweetness makes my life's bitter moments worth tolerating.

What makes me a good husband is having a great wife like you. I am nothing without you. HAPPY BIRTHDAY.

Yours

Vinod"

The poignant letter elicited tears from those who heard it, a testament to the raw and unfiltered emotions woven into its fabric. In the embrace of familial bonds, everyone joined in a collective hug, especially the birthday queen, enveloped in the warmth of love.

Yet, as joy overflowed, a shadow of wisdom lingered—a reminder that the cycle of life encompasses both light and dark, happiness and sorrows. "Never be so happy or never show to others that you are very happy because there is sorrow after happiness and there is dark after the light," a timeless truth echoed through the celebration.

In the quietude of our home, the phone's ring pierced through the air, heralding news that would intertwine joy with uncertainty.

"Didi, there is good news." Babli's voice resonated through the receiver one day.

"Tell me, just now. I can't wait," Laxmi implored, her curiosity piqued.

"We have fixed the wedding of Abhishek," Babli announced.

"Congratulations! This is really good news. Who's the girl?" Laxmi inquired; her excitement palpable.

"You know her, didi," Babli teased.

"I know her! What's her name?" Laxmi asked with surprise.

"You remember, you accompanied me to her home in Kalkaji to stitch some of your suits," Babli revealed.

"Yes, that's Devika."

"Yes, didi."

A cascade of questions tumbled from Laxmi's lips, curious to unravel the unexpected connection between Abhishek and Devika.

"Today I went there for some work. Her mother was talking about the wedding of her daughter," Babli narrated.

"And then?" Laxmi prodded, eager to unearth the unfolding tale.

Babli recounted their conversation:

"The boy is in front of you, and you are not looking at him," Babli urged Devika's mother.

"Whom are you talking about?" Devika's mother inquired.

"I am talking about my son Abhishek," Babli declared.

"Yes, he is a good boy, and I also know your family very well. Is it possible?" Devika's mother pondered.

"We have to talk to the children. If they are agreeable, we will talk further," Babli responded.

"You have eliminated all my worries. I pray to God that both will agree," Devika's mother expressed her hopes.

"I will talk to Abhishek, and you talk to Devika. Let's see," Babli suggested.

"Then have they agreed?" Laxmi questioned.

"Yes, didi, that's why I am calling you," Babli shared joyfully.

"We are planning to go to their home for the Roka ceremony. In our culture, only parents have to go for this small ceremony. Poonam and Naresh will accompany us," she informed.

"All the best and congratulations again," Laxmi conveyed her warm wishes.

As the news reverberated through the household, I received a call from Laxmi.

"Listen, there was a call from Babli. There is good news," she relayed to me.

"What's the news? Tell me," I prompted.

"Abhishek's wedding has been fixed," she revealed, narrating the story she had just heard.

"I will congratulate Manoj," I decided.

"Yes, call him up. I will also congratulate him," Laxmi responded.

The ensuing conversations echoed with joy and felicitations, reminiscent of the celebrations when Prerna's wedding had been announced. However, this time, the pain was less acute, softened by the lack of expectation.

A few days before Abhishek's marriage, an unexpected shadow darkened our door.

"I am not feeling well, Vicky," Laxmi disclosed.

Concern etched Vicky's face as he probed, "What are you feeling? I will talk to the doctor."

"Whenever I stand up and take a few steps, my breath becomes heavy, and I feel suffocated," she admitted.

"I will take an appointment with the doctor," Vicky reassured.

"Doctor says that we have to do some tests, and then he will check them," Vicky reported after consulting with the medical expert. "I will call the lab people at home tomorrow morning."

The next day, with an air of trepidation, Vicky and Laxmi visited the doctor, awaiting the verdict concealed within the test reports.

"What's the report?" Laxmi inquired anxiously.

"I can't understand. We are going to the doctor. He will tell what is to be done," Vicky responded, his voice carrying an undertone of concern.

"I am getting ready," Laxmi replied, her mind racing with myriad thoughts.

"Is everything OK, doctor?" Vicky queried once they were in the doctor's presence.

"I think we will have to do angiography," the doctor revealed.

"But she is not feeling any pain?" Vicky sought clarification.

"It is not necessary that every time we feel pain whenever there is some blockage," the doctor explained.

"OK, doctor, please go ahead."

During the angiography, the doctor delivered an unexpected proclamation, "Again, we have to put a stent."

"Do whatever is the best for her," Vicky consented.

Babli and Manoj rushed to the hospital, offering words of solace and encouragement.

"Don't worry; everything will be alright," Manoj assured.

"I talked to her yesterday. She was looking alright," Babli shared.

"Yes, she was feeling some suffocation," Vicky confided.

"Anyhow, we have reached the right place. She will be alright," I reassured.

"Can I attend the wedding?" Laxmi queried.

"Yes, sure, we will take you along. Jijaji is going to Ahmedabad, and you are staying with us because Vicky and Priyanka are going for a night to celebrate their anniversary," Babli informed.

While Shalu, Deepak, and I were scheduled to attend a conference in Ahmedabad, the timing coincided with the Chowki at Manoj's place. With nobody at home, Laxmi found refuge in the warmth of Babli's household.

"We will not go anywhere for celebration and remain with mummy," Priyanka and Vicky declared.

"No worries, Vicky. We will take care of didi," Babli assured.

"All the programmes of the wedding were solemnised happily and peacefully. However, Laxmi was feeling very weak and sat on the chair during the whole wedding celebration. Everybody met her and asked about her wellness.

As the sands of time flowed, Laxmi gradually regained her strength. The spectre of uncertainty began to fade, replaced by the familiar cadence of everyday life.

One day, as the world tuned in to Prime Minister Modi's address, a collective hush fell over our home, anticipating words that would echo through the annals of history.

"Brothers & Sisters, I have to make a very important announcement today. As you all know, Covid-19 is spreading very fast these days."

The message unfolded, urging a collective pause—a Janta curfew to break the relentless chain of the pandemic. The edict culminated in a symbolic act, a synchronous beating of steel plates and the illumination of earthen lamps.

The shockwave of this unprecedented announcement echoed through our lives, a reminder that even in the cocoon of familial bliss, the larger tapestry of the world could cast its shadows upon us.

In the wake of an unforeseen storm, life took an unexpected turn, propelling us into a realm unknown. Four days metamorphosed into an indefinite lockdown, enveloping us in a cocoon of uncertainty. The world outside ceased to exist, leaving behind shuttered offices, silent schools, and deserted streets. An unfamiliar sense of panic gripped us, as the news of the invisible enemy, Corona, spread like wildfire. Renowned doctors became our guides, offering daily advisories on the dos and don'ts of navigating this uncharted territory. The fear of isolation haunted us, the very idea of segregating an infected person sending shivers down our collective spine.

Quarantine – a term alien to us until late March 2020, suddenly permeated our lives. Reflecting on the past, I pondered over the stark contrast between the eras - the pre-1990 joint-family epoch and the post-1990 nuclear family era.

In the pre-1990 era, our homes were bustling with life, characterised by limited space and abundant hearts. Joint families thrived in modest accommodations, where rooms were not designated as bedrooms, and belongings were shared without hesitation. In this communal haven, every room belonged to everyone, and our shared spaces knew no boundaries. A single toilet catered to the needs of a large family, and nights often unfolded on the roof, filled with shared laughter and camaraderie.

The post-1990 era marked a shift towards isolation. Prosperity ushered in larger homes for smaller families, giving rise to the concept of designated bedrooms, bathrooms, and personal spaces. The shift was palpable, as the collective became compartmentalised into individual territories – my bedroom, my washroom, my TV, my AC. The seeds of isolation were sown, germinating into a culture of self-imposed quarantine. Ironically, we had unwittingly practiced social distancing long before it became a medical directive.

The untidy surroundings of yesteryears hid hearts that were pure, welcoming, and resilient. Fast forward to today, with tidy surroundings, our hearts have grown cluttered. Our once expansive homes now echo with solitude, as blood relations struggle to coexist under the same roof.

A moment of introspection beckons. Have we not cultivated the very isolation that now encircles us? We trained our children to guard their belongings, discouraged sharing, and instilled the ethos of individualism. The doctor's advice to isolate ourselves, or practice "quarantine," should not elicit surprise, for we have been treading this path for over 3 decades.

The lockdown's initial charm, offering a unique opportunity to spend time with family, gradually faded into anxiety and uncertainty. The extended lockdown periods stretched on, creating a culinary revolution within homes. From kulchas to pizzas, from roasted pineapples to besan ladoos, housemakers became culinary maestros. Yet, the repetitive cycle wore thin, leaving fatigue in its wake.

As lockdown restrictions lifted, a new normal emerged, yet fear lingered. Schools remained deserted, places of worship stood silent, and uncertainty shrouded every decision.

"Papa, I told you about the ATS flat in Gurgaon on Dwarka Expressway," Shalu announced during our visit to some customers.

"Has the possession been granted?" I inquired.

"Yes, we want to do interiors," Shalu responded.

"Are you planning to shift?" I questioned.

"No, it will be a gathering and party at home," she explained. "Deepak agreed."

As the day of Greh Pravesh approached, excitement permeated the air. Shalu, the architect of this family haven, orchestrated a celebration that mirrored her love for family. The warmth and laughter echoed in the expansive rooms, symbolic of the bond that had transcended the physical boundaries of a house.

"Mausi-Nani and mummy, you have to perform," Krish insisted on another occasion.

"What performance?" Shalu asked.

"I am playing a song, and you both will perform," Krish declared.

And so, Shalu and Babli, embracing the roles of 'Surili Sisters,' swayed to the rhythm of "Damadam Mast Kalandar." Laughter echoed, bonding deepened, and for a moment, the walls witnessed a performance that transcended the boundaries of everyday life.

Such was the sanctuary that Shalu cultivated – a space where familial bonds are nurtured, celebrations abound, and laughter reigns supreme. In the tapestry of life, these moments became threads, weaving a story of love, togetherness, and resilience.

In the ebbing tides of society's restrictions, a sense of liberation beckoned, casting its spell on everyone. The world, emerging from a prolonged slumber, was awash with the fervour of vacation plans. Our family, too, succumbed to the enchantment, charting a course for a brief sojourn to the untamed splendours of Jim Corbett – a retreat that would weave memories lasting a lifetime.

As the year drew to a close, Shalu, with the air of an orchestrator, proclaimed, "mummy and papa, you all have to come here on 31st December to celebrate New Year." However, Laxmi, matriarch of our familial haven, voiced her reservations, "Shalu, it doesn't look nice to come to your place, eat there, and spend the night. I feel embarrassed. Priyanka and Vicky will come. There's a New Year programme in our society, you know."

Undeterred, Shalu, in her customary authoritative tone, countered, "I don't know anything, mummy. You have to come and spend the night also. My Mother-in-law told me specifically to call all of you."

The die was cast, and so we found ourselves immersed in the festivities, bidding adieu to a tumultuous 2020 with hopes that 2021 would bring solace and joy. The New Year dawned with a question lingering in every mind – would the anticipated blessings manifest?

With the arrival of February, Vicky, ever the harbinger of celebratory plans, revealed, "mummy, this is your 43rd wedding anniversary. We have planned a trip to Jim Corbett or any other place of your choice. We haven't gone anywhere for vacation for a long time. Please tell me."

Laxmi, practical and cautious, raised concerns about extravagant expenses, to which Vicky responded reassuringly, "Don't you worry, mummy. We will arrange everything – myself and didi."

The familial caravan expanded its horizons, encompassing not only Shalu, Krish, and us but also Manoj, Babli, Abhishek, and Devika. Shalu, with her characteristic authority, declared, "Uncle, we are going to Jim Corbett to celebrate mummy and papa's wedding anniversary. We mean you, Babli didi, Abhishek, and Devika. This I am telling you and not asking."

And so, the convoy embarked, 2 cars traversing the roads, carrying the vibrancy of the younger generation and the wisdom of the senior citizens. Laughter echoed as Manoj quipped, "We will prove who is the senior citizen."

The celebration reached its crescendo with a live musical performance, the singer serenading us with the soulful strains of "O sathi re." A jubilant atmosphere, complemented by singing and dancing, enveloped the gathering. Shalu's voice cut through the revelry as she announced, "Come on, the couple, cake has come." The joyous congregation joined in cutting the cake, accompanied by a congratulatory serenade.

Amidst the celebration, a curious guest approached, eager to unravel the longevity of our companionship. "How many years have you two been together?" he inquired, making a shrewd guess.

With a playful banter, we revealed, "It's our 43rd wedding anniversary."

The guest, in awe, marvelled at our youthfulness. "You both don't look so old," he exclaimed. Undeterred, I declared, "Our life has just begun. We will celebrate our 50th anniversary in a grander way."

As the festivities wove a tapestry of cherished memories, the question lingered – could we indeed celebrate our 50th anniversary, or was it an ephemeral dream? The trip to Jim Corbett, bathed in the glow of celebration, etched itself as the most memorable chapter in the book of our lives.

The evening hung in contemplative stillness as I pondered the mysteries of destiny with my friend. "If everything in life is predestined, where is the scope to use our intelligence?" I mused.

"Whoever told you that everything is destined? Nothing is destined," he responded, his eyes reflecting a profound wisdom. "It is just that unconsciously you have made yourself into a certain possibility. You create certain tendencies within you with your unconsciousness, and according to the tendencies, you keep moving in that direction. The destiny you are talking about is something you created unconsciously; you can also create it consciously."

As the weight of his words settled in my mind, uncertainty lingered. "We didn't know what our destiny was after some time," I confessed.

Days unfolded, each bearing its own tale. A call from Devika, one that seemed ordinary, held the essence of a fateful summons. "Mausaji, you have to come on 4th April on the occasion of papa's birthday," she declared, an invitation tinged with anticipation.

"Sure beta, we will reach," I assured. Devika extended her invitation to others, but I dismissed the need, stating, "No need. You told me, that's enough. We will be there on time."

Shalu inquired about my plans, "papa, are you going to Noida on 4th?" She grappled with uncertainty, "I don't know. Prerna is not here. I don't know how they can celebrate without her?"

"It's their choice, Shalu. Please come; we will also meet," I encouraged.

The gathering, seemingly ordinary, unfolded with joy and surprises. Prerna and Ankit's unexpected arrival adorned the occasion, infusing it with an unexpected charm.

Little did we know that fate had orchestrated this meeting for a poignant purpose. Regret, a potent emotion, crept in – a feeling of sadness, guilt, or disappointment over occurrences or actions, a bee buzzing incessantly within the confines of our thoughts.

The narrative took a sombre turn as Laxmi, after days of fever, faced a grave health crisis. The ominous shadow of the pandemic loomed. The Covid test, initially negative, yielded an unforeseen positive result, coupled with dwindling oxygen levels.

As Vicky, Priyanka, and Laxmi prepared to leave for the hospital, I could only utter, "Come soon." The emergency Ward awaited, and I held my breath for the news.

"Papa, mummy is in the emergency ward," Vicky's voice relayed.

"Is everything OK?" I asked, my heart echoing my unease.

"Yes, again they conducted a Covid test, and it is positive. Oxygen is low, but they are giving her oxygen. She is alright otherwise," reassured Vicky.

The unexpected twist unravelled further. "But yesterday, Covid was negative," I expressed my bewilderment.

"Don't know, papa," was the only response.

Amid the tumultuous events, the impending question lingered – would they admit her? Vicky's updates painted a grim picture – an ICU bed was indispensable. Dr. Parneesh, relentless in his efforts, sought admission, but beds in ICU proved elusive.

"I will also try. One of my ex-colleagues is in Apollo," I offered a glimmer of hope.

"Please don't worry. She will come home soon," I reassured Vicky, the gravity of the situation etched in every word.

The journey through uncertainty unfolded as Vicky reported, "I got confirmation from Yashoda Hospital to get an ICU bed. Shall I go there?"

A tinge of doubt lingered, "Is it a good hospital?" I queried.

"Not of that standard, but under the circumstances, we have no choice," Vicky admitted.

"OK then, please take her to Yashoda. In the meantime, if I receive a call from Apollo, I will inform you. That's a better choice," I proposed.

"OK papa, I am getting her relieved," Vicky declared.

"OK," I responded, each word laced with the weight of the unknown future.

The weight of the impending blunder pressed upon us, a fog of uncertainty clouding our senses. The sole fixation in our minds was the urgent need to secure her a spot in the ICU of any available hospital.

"Papa, she got the bed in Yashoda," Vicky conveyed, his voice a mix of relief and concern.

"Please take care of her," I responded, my mind grappling with the limitations imposed by the Covid ward.

"I can't go there because of the Covid ward," he confessed, a tangible worry evident in his words.

"No worries, you know the owner of the hospital. Please talk to her. They should take care of her," I suggested, extending a desperate plea for reassurance.

"I have to come back, papa. Nobody can stay in the Covid ward," he declared, his resolve firm.

"Then come back. Just counsel your mummy. We have never left her alone in the hospital. She must have anxiety," I urged, recognising the importance of emotional support.

"Yes, papa, I talked to her. It's a matter of 4-5 days only. As soon as her oxygen level becomes normal, she will be relieved," he assured, attempting to infuse optimism into the grim situation.

"Come home then."

"Papa, I am not feeling well. I have called for an RT-PCR test tomorrow, and hence I am isolating myself," Vicky informed upon his return from the hospital.

"OK, please take care. Priyanka will prepare dinner for you. Please take medicine and rest," I instructed, concerned weaving through my words.

"I am positive," Vicky revealed after receiving his test report the next day.

"I have to be quarantined for 14 days. Don't come in my room," he declared, marking the beginning of a challenging period.

"Please look after yourself and don't worry. We are talking to the doctor to prescribe medicines for you," I reassured, navigating through the uncertainty.

The days unfolded, laden with difficulty. Priyanka, too, succumbed to the illness, her health compromised. Laxmi was in the hospital, and Shalu couldn't join us due to the pandemic.

As 2 days passed, Vicky's condition deteriorated, body ache and fever exacerbating his distress. "I am taking rest," Priyanka informed me after 2 days.

"Are you alright?" I inquired.

"It seems I am suffering from a fever," she confessed.

"We will call for an RT-PCR test tomorrow because it becomes necessary now," I decided.

"OK."

The house echoed with the revelation of Priyanka's positive result. "Go in the same room now since both are positive," I directed. "This way you will take care of Vicky also."

"OK, papa."

"How is mummy now?" Shalu called and asked.

"She is not well, Shalu. Vicky and Priyanka are also not well. What should I do?" I expressed my distress.

"You may go to ATS home when mummy comes home. I will tell the maid to prepare food for you," Shalu suggested.

"I can't live there alone," I confessed.

"OK, in that case, since you are negative, I, along with Krish, will go there with you and remain there till all is well," she offered.

"OK, let mummy come first," I said.

"I am going for the 2nd vaccination dose, Vicky," I informed him after a week.

"OK, papa, go there with lots of protection," he advised.

I ventured to Max Patparganj for the 2nd vaccination dose, the weight of the pandemic clinging to every step. Gratitude swelled within me for those who extended their care during our crisis. My incapacity in the kitchen left us reliant on others for sustenance, with food arriving from various sources, notably from Harishankar Ji's home.

"Babli and Manoj insisted daily to send food, but I told them that the same is coming from Harishankar Ji's home," I recounted.

"Papa, I received a call from Devika. She wants to send food today," Vicky relayed one day.

"No, please deny. It doesn't look good. I refused Manoj also," I insisted.

"I said the same, but she is adamant," he explained.

"Please call her and refuse, and say thanks again," I urged.

She sent food, not once but twice. Similar gestures of kindness flowed from Akash, a childhood friend of Vicky, who sent food twice during those trying days.

I remain indebted to these benevolent souls who stood with us in our hour of need, expressing my heartfelt thanks for their noble assistance.

"I am still feeling feverish, Vicky," I confided after 2 days.

"I am booking the Covid test slot for you. Please go there and get the test done," he instructed.

"What is the use of testing when I got the 2nd vaccine dose also?" I questioned.

"It's better, papa. What's the harm? We all will be relaxed if it is negative," he reasoned.

"OK, I will go. Please book."

As the duty of calling Laxmi persisted, her loneliness became increasingly palpable. However, after a week, she voiced her frustration, expressing a singular desire – "Please take me home."

"Vicky, please talk to the doctor. When will mummy be discharged?" I implored.

"I already talked, papa. She still needs oxygen. Either we arrange an oxygen concentrator at home, or she will remain there," he revealed.

"She is getting restless day by day. I want to bring her home, come what may," I declared.

"If you want to kill her, please get her discharged," he retorted.

The words hung in the air, a heavy silence settling in as the harsh reality of our situation unfolded.

It became my responsibility to cater to the needs of the children, providing food, tea, and fruits, as I found myself the sole inhabitant of an eerily quiet house.

"I am also tested positive," Shalu shared one day.

"Take care, Shalu. Manoj will send the required medicines to you also," I assured.

"There is breathlessness, papa," she admitted, her voice betraying discomfort.

"Please take the medicines on time and also the nebuliser and steam thrice a day," I advised.

"I am doing the same, papa, but there is severe pain," she confided.

"You have to bear, Shalu. You have to manage because nobody can come to your room," I acknowledged.

"I know. Please take care of mummy," she requested.

"Sir, I got a bed in Max Saket for Shalini as she is breathless and short of oxygen," Deepak called one day.

"That's good. Now she will be treated well," I said.

"Let's hope," he responded.

"Please take care of yourself also," I urged, the uncertainty of the situation looming over our every interaction.

The relentless quest for an oxygen concentrator echoed through the corridors of despair, a desperate search spanning cities and even reaching across borders to Dubai, each effort met with the harsh reality of unavailability.

"Sharma ji, I received a concentrator, but it is 7 litres, as against 10 litres as suggested by the doctor," Manoj's voice reached me one day.

"I am sending the same to you. Please take that along and show it to the doctor," he suggested, his efforts in arranging medicines and injections proving to be a crucial lifeline for the children.

"OK."

Navigating the intricacies of a pandemic, I found myself grappling with the overwhelming responsibility of managing everything alone. My mind, laden with distress, sought solace in the solitude of the drawing room or the quiet confines of my room.

The scheduled Covid test became a stark revelation the next day.

"You are positive, papa," Vicky conveyed, unravelling the unexpected twist even after my second vaccine.

"Yes, papa."

"Then, you people come out of your room. We all are positive, and let's sit together," I suggested, marking a reunion after an extended period.

"Manoj is sending a concentrator of 7 litres tomorrow. We have to go to show the same to the doctor," I informed Vicky.

"OK, we will go," he agreed.

Amidst the waiting, with Vicky enduring health concerns, a critical call brought Shalu's voice through a video call.

"Papa, where is mummy? I want to talk to her right now," she implored.

"Yes, sure," I replied.

"Have you got the concentrator?" she asked.

"Yes, we got it and brought it here to show to the doctor. If he approves, we will get her home," I explained.

"OK."

"Talk to mummy," Vicky handed the phone to Laxmi, initiating a heartfelt conversation.

"Doctor, we have arranged this concentrator," we informed him when he visited Laxmi.

"No, this is not the right one. You have to arrange a 10-litre concentrator," he specified, setting us on a quest for the suitable machine.

"OK, we will try to arrange," I assured.

"This concentrator is not suitable, and hence we are arranging another one," I communicated to Laxmi, who clung to the hope of imminent relief.

"I don't know when I will go home," she expressed her deep anxiety.

"Don't be nervous; we are trying. We will take you along as soon as we arrange the concentrator," I reassured, navigating through the uncertainty.

Reflecting on a trip to Vaishno Devi, a memory surfaced, showcasing Laxmi's discomfort in solitude even for an hour. Now, the lady who couldn't sit alone for an hour was confined to a hospital bed for 23 days. Helplessness took its toll, and tears flowed freely.

Vicky's health teetered on the edge, prompting the doctor to declare the urgent need for an ICU bed. Despite our best efforts, the circumstances thwarted our attempts. In retrospect, the unavailability of an ICU bed might have been a saving grace.

"Papa, one concentrator is available in Mumbai, but he wants an advance of Rs. 1.80 lakhs," Vicky relayed one day.

"When will he send the same?" I inquired.

"We will receive it after 2 days. He will send it by courier," he explained.

"Please transfer the amount immediately," I insisted.

"It can be risky, papa," he cautioned.

"At least there is a hope of receiving the same. Please transfer," I urged.

"OK."

"Call him and ask which courier is going to deliver to us. We will send our person to that courier in Mumbai and get it expedited," I strategised.

"Hello, this is Ankit (Vicky). By which courier are you sending the machine?" Vicky inquired.

"So sorry Ankit, we tried to send, but the Maharashtra Government restricted the movement of any concentrator to other states," came the response.

"Then?"

"I can't help; I have to refund your money," he conceded.

Fate seemed to toy with us, thwarting our earnest efforts to secure the machine at any cost. The looming question of how and when we would bring Laxmi back hung heavily over our minds.

"Sir, Shalini is not feeling well. Nobody is coming there to treat her and give medicines. Can you talk to the doctor and arrange?" Deepak's plea reached me one day.

"Yes, I will talk," I affirmed.

Now, my duty extended beyond talking to the doctor for Shalu; it also included consoling Laxmi over the phone. But was it really that simple?

"Shalini is not feeling well. Both of my brothers are going to the hospital," Deepak informed over a call.

"I am going there and will meet the doctor. Don't worry," I assured.

"Vicky, I am going to Max. Shalu is not feeling well," I informed.

"Today I am feeling a bit better and will go along," he said.

"Please take rest. I will see," I said.

"No papa, I would also like to meet didi," he insisted.

"OK, but don't take stress. Everything will be fine," I consoled.

"Have you met the doctor?" I asked Deepak's brothers.

"No, they didn't let us meet her," they replied.

"Let me arrange something," I proposed.

Talking to the security supervisor, known to us, I orchestrated a meeting between Vicky and Shalu to gauge the situation. Despite his own health concerns, Vicky spent more than 3 hours in the Covid ward, sitting on the stairs.

"How is she?" We all asked when he returned.

"She is crying, papa. She cannot bear the pain of the tight oxygen mask on her face," he disclosed.

"Didn't you tell her that this is necessary?" I questioned.

"I tried to counsel her, but she is not able to tolerate the same," he confessed.

The heaviness of the moment hung in the air; our eyes moist with helplessness. The resilient girl who never walked barefoot on the ground now endured unimaginable pain, and we, her family, stood powerless.

Returning home, Vicky lay down in the car, fatigued and mentally drained by the conditions that befell his beloved sister. The wheels of our lives turned, each rotation echoing the harsh reality of our shared struggles.

"Sharma ji, I talked to a person who has the concentrator of specifications of our requirement. I am going there," Manoj's voice echoed through the phone after 2 days.

"That's good news, Manoj. Can I come along? Shall I send money?" I asked in excitement.

"Don't worry, I am carrying cash with me. I will call you. You and Vicky should reach the hospital and process for discharge. I will reach with the machine," he said.

"OK, we are waiting for your call," I said.

"I got the machine. It matches the specifications also. Please reach the hospital," he informed.

"OK."

"Vicky, please get ready immediately. We are going to the hospital to get Laxmi discharged. Manoj is reaching there with the machine," I told.

"That's good news, papa. I am getting ready," he also got excited.

"Sir, I received a call from the hospital. Shalini has got a heart attack, and doctors are trying to get her revived," Deepak called as we were getting ready.

"What do you mean by reviving?" I asked.

"I don't know. Going to the hospital," he said.

"Please don't worry. Everything will be alright; I am also reaching there," I told.

"What happened, papa?" Priyanka came running.

"Shalu has got a heart attack; we are going there," I informed.

"What?" She screamed and ran towards the temple for prayer.

"Sir, Shalini is no more!" Deepak called me after 5 minutes.

There was explosive silence for 2 minutes.

"What? It cannot be possible. We are on the way to the hospital. I will talk to the doctor," I said.

"Manoj, please don't go to the hospital. Shalu is no more," I told.

"What are you talking about? How can it be possible? I am coming to Max just now," he said.

"OK."

"Abhishek, Shalu is no more; please take Babli to Vasundhara. Priyanka is alone there," I called Abhishek.

"What? Are you in senses? It cannot be possible," he shouted.

"I am very well in senses. Please bring Babli," I said. "Also, please talk to Laxmi. Tell her that the machine has been arranged but it has to be kept in isolation for 24 hours, and we will get her discharged tomorrow positively."

"Don't worry, 2. I will do what you said," he still was in shock.

"No papa, No papa, No papa!" Vicky screamed the whole way.

"Where is Shalu?" I was lying on the floor crying profusely.

Vicky ran towards the gate, pushing the gatekeeper.

"I also want to see Shalu," I was screaming. Nobody listened to me. Everybody was devastated.

What should I tell Laxmi when she returns back home? She will collapse. My whole life has been ruined. I was weeping badly.

My little child Krish. I immediately hugged him tight. He was also there in the hospital.

It seemed somebody stabbed me in my heart with full force. What should I do now?

"Where is the doctor? I would like to talk to him. How can it be possible? No, not at all. She is still alive. Doctor, can you please check again." I was murmuring in a slow voice – slow because I was screaming in a loud voice the whole way from home to the hospital.

"Vicky, have you met Shalu?" Immediately, I ran towards Vicky.

"Yes papa, I met her just now," he said.

"How is she? She is alright now. What did the doctor say?" I bombarded him with questions.

"Nothing is left papa. She is no more," Vicky was inconsolable.

"Please take me to the doctor. I will talk to him. He will check her again," I lied down on the floor.

"Please calm down papa," Vicky was trying to console me, still crying hard.

How can I? Nothing has been left in my life now. What should I tell Laxmi? She will collapse even before hearing the full incident.

Let's take her to the cremation. I have settled the bill. I was listening to these words as if somebody was talking to me from very far.

Like a robot, I followed them.

"Please show us the face," Deepak was requesting the ambulance driver.

"I can't, sir. I will lose my job," he said.

"Nobody will see. Please, for the last time, I beg you," Deepak insisted.

"OK sir, don't request me like this. I am also a human being," he agreed.

"Just see here," the driver pulled the zip of the coffin.

"Oh my God. My Gudia is going on the last visit. I am left alone," I was weeping like Hell.

"Don't be so devastated, papa. We have to take care of mummy also," Vicky was counselling me.

"Yes!"

I bid goodbye to my little child twice in my life. First at the time of her marriage and second now. How unlucky a person I am?

The loss of a child is incredibly, deeply painful. I know this much, grief for a child singes your heart and tears at your soul. Such grief is a lifelong journey. There are no easy answers. There are no easy outs.

My child died. Really, she was a young adult. She was just 42. What followed? Shock, chaos, denial, pain, remorse, and suffering like I had never felt before. My world turned upside down and sideways. It shook me by the throat. Grief held me hostage.

And I have come to know this: one of the only things that helps a parent out of deepest grief is to connect with others who likewise deeply grieve. Immediately a thought came into my mind. What would happen if I disclosed this in front of Laxmi? If I am heartbroken, she is the mother. Oh God, give me the strength to face her.

In that spirit of love, connection, and outreach, I give the only thing I have to offer another mother during the worst moments of her life: the hard-earned and heartfelt lessons I have learned after losing a child.

When a child dies, their beautiful, kind, and inspiring presence is bodily absent from this life. This unthinkable loss will permeate your life in so many ways. You will live every day absorbing and managing her absence, but also feeling her presence. Grief for your child will ebb, flow, and change, and you will learn to incorporate it into your mind, body, and spirit. Her life is and continues to be part of your own. You will never get past or 'recover' from the trauma, but you may learn to build the monumental loss into your own continuing life.

The child's life holds deep meaning and purpose. Your child is and remains your daughter or your son. Their smile, compassion, mischievousness, intelligence, athleticism — these were real and present in life, and they are real and present even after a child's death. Though it's hard to understand the why of a child dying, it's possible to hold onto the beauty and joy our children gave the world even in the short time they were here. Their life was a gift — and their light continues to shine.

Grief for a child may be the deepest grief we experience. Grief is unavoidable. It is the price we pay for loving deeply. Mourning a child encompasses every part of you, mind, heart, body, soul. You will experience the loss, absorb the loss, and relive the loss. You will be carried by grief, and it will carry you. Be careful of people who want you to believe definite ideas about grief, that it progresses, comes in phases, or is predictable. Trust yourself. Trust your heart. Trust your grief, which is your love for your child, continued.

Grief is not an arrow. Grief is not linear. Time becomes different. You live in a world that embraces paradox, all at once, you are steeped in the past, the present, and the now. You walk in a new world, one wherein your child is absent, and one where she is omnipresent. The straight arrow of time becomes bent. You walk in ambiguity, but this complex world becomes more navigable. Trust yourself as you walk.

Trauma is a disconnected disorder that divides us from ourselves as well as others. Deep and traumatic grief can bring deep connections as well as deep disruptions. You will be disappointed in people who are not or cannot be there for you. At the same time, you will be strengthened and encouraged by those who show up. Often, these are people you never imagined. Beware of too much isolation. Accept help when it is offered. Guard your heart, but also leave a window open. You may find the deepest connections of your life during tragedy. Be open to new friendships with people who have been through similar experiences: they will enrich and support you and love you as you are.

Some days, your sorrow will seem too much. Some days, you will wish to sink into forgetfulness. This life will seem too sad, too cruel, too overbearing to want to remain here. You will feel that the easiest way is out. Death can seem warm and welcoming — after all, your child is there. Understand that you will feel this way, and it's fine. It's not much discussed, but many bereaved parents have felt this draw towards death. It comes and goes and may do so for the rest of your life.

Trauma changes us. Your beliefs, ideas, values, principles, faith all these and more are touched or torn by the depth of your sorrow. Of all the life lessons that come from losing a child, this one rule supreme: our love for our beloved children lives on. Past tragedy, past grief, past death: love endures. As parents, we bond with our child at their birth. As bereaved parents, we retain the right to that bond even after they've died. We loved them fiercely then; we love them as fiercely now. That light — that love — lives on. It illuminates the days when our children lived and laughed and loved with all their hearts. And it lights the days we recall, remember, and relish their joy and love and hugs even after they are gone.

You loved your child the moment she was born. You love her now on this tragic day. Your love endures; it will carry you and your family, always.

"Are you ready, papa?" Vicky's voice broke the morning silence the next day.

"Yes, let's go." We were on our way to the cremation ground to collect the remains of Shalu, from where Deepak and his brothers would depart for Haridwar.

What a cruel test of life. Krish, who had never let go of his mother's hand, was now cradling her remains in his lap. Unfortunately, it was Mother's Day.

We left the site as soon as Deepak moved. Now, we were bracing ourselves for another test of patience. We needed to reach the hospital to complete the formalities for Laxmi's discharge.

After a quick bath, we reached the hospital, accompanied by Babli and Manoj.

"You go to Laxmi while we meet the doctor," I instructed Babli and Priyanka.

"Sure," they responded, a mix of excitement and fear evident in their faces. The truth of Shalu's demise was a heavy burden to carry.

"Have you made arrangements at home?" Abhishek inquired.

"What arrangement? The oxygen concentrator is with us," I replied.

"What if we have to switch off the concentrator after some time?" he questioned.

"Yes, you are right. We forgot," I admitted.

"Don't worry; I have arranged for a cylinder. After some time, we will switch to the cylinder," he suggested.

"I think we should go home first to make such arrangements before she reaches," Vicky proposed.

"OK, please go, Vicky, and Priyanka, along with Babli. Manoj and I are here to take care," I said.

After completing numerous formalities, we were ready to head home that night.

"Please bring her along with the oxygen cylinder," I told the nurse.

"Yes, of course."

"Please put your foot in the ambulance," I asked Laxmi.

It was a surprise to all of us when she couldn't move her leg at all.

After numerous attempts, she was finally settled in the ambulance.

"Priyanka, we will reach within 10 minutes," I called from the ambulance, accompanying Laxmi.

"Please tell Shalu that I am reaching home," Laxmi requested.

It was challenging to remain calm at that stage.

"Shalu has been hospitalised with an oxygen mask on her face; how can she talk?" I said.

"OK."

We transformed our home into a makeshift hospital, complete with a full-time nurse, an electric bed, an air mattress, 3 50-litre cylinders, 2 oxygen concentrators, and more. But our eyes and faces betrayed a deep sadness.

It was the hardest time of our lives. We couldn't grieve for our little child. What fate! We ate, laughed, and looked normal in front of her.

Laxmi, too, was not fully aware. She slept most of the time.

"Listen, please send back this nurse and instead call Bimla," Laxmi requested one day when she was awake. Bimla was more like a family member than a maid.

"What's wrong with this nurse? She is doing all the chores," I said.

"No, Bimla is better than this nurse. I will be alright if you call her," she said.

"OK, we will call her. Now you take rest," I said.

Bimla had entered our lives during my heart surgery. Babli had sent her to take care of the family because Vicky's wedding was approaching, Laxmi had undergone angioplasty a month back, and all the pending shopping work needed attention.

"Didi, I am sending one lady, Bimla, to take care of the family," Babli had said.

"Can we trust her? If we leave home to go shopping, is she honest?" Laxmi inquired.

"Yes, didi. I have known her for many years," Babli replied.

Bimla took on the responsibility immediately upon her arrival. She even took care of me when nobody was at home.

From then on, whenever we needed support and help, only Bimla came to mind and was called.

She was with us during Vicky's wedding, during Priyanka's 3 sicknesses due to abortion, and whenever we needed a kind, honest, and loyal person.

I don't know when and how she became a family member, and now Laxmi was eager to call her to take care. Unfortunately, due to the pandemic, we couldn't call her at that time.

"Why don't you talk to us?" Babli asked Laxmi when she noticed Laxmi was not talking to anyone after coming back from the hospital.

Laxmi didn't respond.

"I am talking. OK, who am I?" Babli persisted.

"My everything," was the reply.

"You don't know what happened in the hospital," she started talking.

"What?" we asked.

"The nurses there always demotivated me," she said.

"What did they say to you?" I inquired.

"They said that my family left me in the hospital, and I will not return from here," she said.

"But you proved them wrong and came back home," I said.

"Yes, still, it is like a dream," she said.

"Don't worry. You will be alright now," Priyanka reassured her.

"Yes, beta. You people are working very hard," she said.

"Working hard for whom? For our mother only," Priyanka said, and Laxmi started smiling.

We didn't know we were very good actors. Of course, it was the acting we were performing. We were one way in front of Laxmi and completely different in another room. We all cried softly so that she would not know the truth.

"Babli, I want to tell you one thing," Laxmi said one day.

"Tell me, didi," Babli asked.

"You people have made all the arrangements for my treatment, but I will die soon," she said.

"Why are you talking like this?" Babli asked with moist eyes. "You are getting better as the days pass," Babli assured her.

I was feeling very helpless and was terribly remembering Shalu one day while sitting in the drawing room thinking when we will be able to cry in a loud voice and when will we tell this truth to Laxmi.

I started writing to Shalu as this is the only method, I know to express myself and to keep my mind calm.

पापा पापा मुझे ढूंढों । कोई चीटिंग नहीं पापा । आंख बंद करके दस तक गिनों मैं छुप रही हूं ।

हां बेटा 1…. 2…. 3…. 4…… 5…… 6…. 7…… 8…. 9…. 10…. हां बेटा मैं आऊं?? शालू…. शालू…. बेटा जवाब दो । कहां छुपी हो? बेटा इतनी दूर जाकर ना छिपो कि मैं तुम्हें ढूंढ ना सकूं । शालू बेटा जवाब दो…. तुम कुछ बोल क्यों नहीं रही? अब ये चीटिंग है । चलो मैं हार गया …. तुम जीत गई …. अब तो आ जाओ । अब तो वापस आ जाओ ।

मैं जिंदगी भर लिखता रहा । खूब लिखा …. सबके लिए लिखा । कभी कलम नहीं सूखी । आज स्याही के लिए दवात खोली तो वो भी खाली । आज शायद पहली बार स्याही की जगह आंसू से लिख रहा हूं । पता नहीं अपना लिखा ख़ुद पढ़ पाऊंगा या नहीं ।

"शालू कहां छिप गई जाकर । कहीं नहीं मिल रही ।"

"बेटा वापस आ जाओ । तुम्हारा पापा थक गया बेटा । आकर मुझसे लिपट जाओ । अब ये लुकाछिपी का खेल और नहीं खेला जाएगा मुझसे । शालू वापस आ जाओ बेटा । शालू…. शालू ।"

"शालू जो मेरी एक आवाज में दौड़ी चली आती थी । मैं बीमार हुआ । अस्पताल में भर्ती हुआ । शालू सब कुछ छोड़कर घंटों मेरे कमरे के बाहर बैठी रहती थी और आज …. आज उसका पापा उसे पुकार रहा है तो पता नहीं क्यों?? शालू बेटा अब तो आ जा"

शालू…. हम सबकी लाडली… हमारे घर की पहली बच्ची…. अपनी दादी की दुलारी…. सब पर दिलो जान से प्यार लुटाने वाली …. पता ही नहीं चला कब बढ़ी हुई और कब हमारे आंगन को पार कर अपने पति के घर चल दी । जो शालू हमारे एक घर की लाडली थी

अब दूसरे घर जाकर एक लाडली बहू …. ख्याल करने वाली पत्नी और ममता से भरी मां बन गई । जिस शालू को हम सब ने एक राजकुमारी की तरह पाला था उस शालू की किस्मत में भी कुछ काटे थे । एक मां होकर उसने अपनी छोटी मासूम बेटी को जाने का दर्द सहा । जब कृष हुआ तो वह इतनी सतर्क हो गई कि कभी कृष को बड़ा ही होने नहीं दिया हमेशा अपनी नजरों के सामने रखा । उसके लालन पालन से लेकर उसकी पढ़ाई तक कभी उसे अपनी नजरों से ओझल होने नहीं दिया और अब …… जब वो हम सबको छोड़कर दूर चली गई है ये भी नहीं देखा कि कृष एकदम से कितना बडा हो गया । 9 मई को मदर्स डे पर वो अपनी मां को कंधे में उठाना चाहता था ….. वो कृष अपनी मां की अस्थियों को गोद में लेकर गंगा में प्रवाहित कर रहा था । शालू मेरे लिए ना सही अपने कृष के लिए वापस आ जाओ । बेटा अब बडा हो गया है…. ताकतवर हो गया है लेकिन इतना बडा नहीं हुआ कि बिना मां के जिन्दगी गुजार पाए ।

जिंदगी में हर दिन कुछ नया करना नया दौड़ना और नए नए सरप्राइज से अपने घर परिवार के लोगों के चेहरों पर मुस्कान बिखेरना । जितना अपने मां बाप का ख्याल रखना उतना ही अपने सास-ससुर की देखभाल करना । अपने भाई के लिए भाभी के लिए हमेशा प्यार लुटाना । अपने हाथों से अपना घरौंदा सजाना और अपने पति दीपक के कंधे से कंधे मिलाकर खड़े रहना । छोटी सी जिंदगी में कितनी पूरी थी शालू - एक बेटी एक बहन एक बहू एक पत्नी और एक मां । इतना ख्याल रखने वाली कि हम सब से बहुत दूर जाकर भी यही सोच रही होगी कि हम लोग दुखी ना हो... रोए ना और जब भी शालू के साथ बिताई जिंदगी के लम्हों को याद करें चेहरे पर एक शांत मुस्कान आए ।

अपने एटीएस वाले घर में जाने के लिए कितनी एक्साइटेड थी घर के लोगों की छोटी से भी छोटी जरूरतों का ख्याल ताकि कहीं कोई कमी ना रह जाए । घर परिवार ही जिसकी दुनिया हो जिनकी खुशी में ही उसकी खुशी हो । ऐसी थी हमारी शालू ।

और घर परिवार ही क्यों सभी नाते रिश्तेदारों की भी लाडली थी शालू । सब से मिलकर खुश होना सब की सलामती की दुआ करना और छोटी से छोटी बातों का ख्याल रखना । हमने भगवान से इतना नहीं मांगा था उससे भी ज्यादा दे गई हम सबको शालू ।

बेटा भगवान के दरवाजे तक पहुंच गई । अब तो उनकी भी लाडली बन गई होगी । पार्थिव यात्रा आर्ट ऑफ लिविंग का ही एक्सटेंशन है । जिस जिंदादिली से जी शालू उसी जिंदादिली से अपनी आखिरी यात्रा पर निकल पड़ी ।

शालू इतना रची बसी है हम सबकी जिंदगी में कि लगता ही नहीं कि वह शरीर से हमसे दूर है । यहीं कहीं आस पास ही है । अभी आएगी और बोलेगी कि पापा मैं आ गई । पक्का यकीन है कि हमारी शालू किसी न किसी रूप में हम सबके जिंदगी में फिर से वापस आएगी.... फिर से हम सबका दिल जीतेगी ... फिर से हम सबको अपना बनाएगी और फिर से.......

आजका लुका छुपी का खेल कुछ अलग है । हम सब की मुस्कान कहीं छुप गई है । लेकिन यह खेल शालू का रचा हुआ है । बहुत ज्यादा देर कहीं छुप सकती है और ना ही हमारी मुस्कान ।

यह वादा है हमारा शालू कि जब भी तुम्हारी याद आएगी हम आंसू नहीं बहाएंगे । जितनी जिंदगी तुम्हारे साथ बिताई है उन लम्हों को याद करेंगे और तुम्हारी याद में मुस्काएंगे । और हां जिस बगिया को तुमने अपने हाथ से बनाया है सजाया है सहारा है उसका भी ख्याल वैसे ही रखेंगे जैसे तुम रखती ।

बहुत हुआ लुका छुपी का खेल । अब तुम हमसे छुप नहीं सकती । तुम्हारा पापा फिर से जीत गया है क्योंकि अब उसने तुम्हें अपने दिल में हमेशा के लिए छुपा लिया है और जब चाहे दिल में झांक कर तुम्हें देख सकता है ।

शालू मेरी शालू ।।

"Papa, mujhe dhoondo. Aankh bund karo, no cheating". "Shalu, where are you?", "I am nowhere," came the plea. I pretended to locate her, finally finding her.

"Cheating, papa, you're cheating. Again, locate me," she challenged.

Of course, I cheated to find her. Today, when I have done no cheating, please call me, Shalu. I am not able to find you anywhere. Please come back and hug me tight. Please, please, please, I urge you.

"Ek Aah Bhari Hogi, Humne Na Suni Hogi, Jaate Jaate Tumne, Aawaz To Di Hogi, Ek Aah Bhari Hogi, Humne Na Suni Hogi, Jaate Jaate Tumne, Aawaz To

Di Hogi, Har Waqt Yahi Hai Ghum, Us Waqt Kahan The Hum, Ho Jab Tum Chale Gaye."

"Dunia se jaane wale jaane chale jaate hain kahan. Koi kaise dhoonde unko nahin kadmon ke bhi nishan."

In my deepest dreams, I could not think about this song for my beloved princess, who left me alone to cry. Fate is such that it snatched our most valuable things from us, and we are feeling helpless. This sudden and shocking loss is overwhelming, but God, in His early plan, prepared a girl 6 years ago to fill Shalu's place. However, there is no replacement for a person like Shalu. She was, is, and will be unique.

From the day of her birth, she lived like a princess, the first child in our home, loved by everyone. She was her dadi's laadli. Marrying a man who fulfilled her every wish, the family she joined loved her until her last breath. She faced a significant hit early in her marriage when her first child, a lovely girl, passed away. This fear prevented her from making Krish independent, and even until her last days, he slept with her. I don't know how he will cope with life now without his mummy. Fate had other plans. Krish took her "asthian" in his lap on Mother's Day 9th May 2021. How he felt at that time, only he knows. He became mature overnight and didn't cry in front of others. I wish God blesses him with the courage to bear this unbearable loss.

I still remember when I was admitted to the hospital for the first time for a small appendix operation. On hearing this, she immediately ran towards the hospital and slipped on the staircase. During my bypass surgery, she used to come early in the morning and leave late at night for the entire 10-12 days. She was so concerned about her parents that a small ailment was significant for her. She was dedicated to her parents-in-law as well, with her own rules—no strings attached. No ifs, ands, or buts.

Thinking about her now, the art of dying must be an extension of the art of living. She lived a life of comfort, but the unwalled joys were the most rewarding. Every facet of her life shone with contentment and tranquillity, brought on by a sense of accomplishment. She never had to yearn for anything. It didn't matter.

Like all mortal beings, there were occasions and reasons for feeling dissatisfied. But she always asked herself, "Is there any need to punish oneself with unhappiness?" This swift banishment of negative thoughts made her certain that, as with the sojourn, the departure from life too would be amidst the surround-sound of pleasure and excitement.

Restless for new experiences, she focused on her dream home "ATS" during her last days, where she wanted her whole family to gather and enjoy. She made everything available there so that nobody in the family would talk about any problems. She was successful in that.

Having said all this, I would like to tell her to go with peace. Tell death, sweetly, to wait a bit while you adjust your pillow just so and snuggle into my chadar for the right degree of warmth. She wasn't worried about settling matters in this world. Material bonds are being united as she gravitates toward her last halt before the final destination.

She hasn't gone anywhere. The little girl who used to run after hearing the suffering of any family member, the girl who forgot her sickness to help others, the girl whose family was her world, the girl who was so innocent that you tell her, and she believes, the girl who was so honest that she couldn't hide anything for a long time. She was fond of giving surprises. She enjoyed seeing us smile. She felt good to see all the family members together. She couldn't tolerate our sufferings. She can't leave our lives. She is still here, counselling us not to cry. Those we love don't go away; they walk beside us — unseen, unheard but always near us, still loved, still missed, and very dear to us. She will definitely come back physically into our lives in a new role. She will again conquer everybody's heart. She will again rule all of us. When she comes back to our lives, it will not be a surprise because we already know it. Wait for that day.

"Papa, I talked to the doctor and shared all the reports of mummy. He was told to have a recent CT report and advised to get her admitted to a good hospital where all her tests will be conducted along with CT," Vicky told me one day as Laxmi's condition was not improving at home.

"Will she agree? She was under trauma for 23 days in Yashoda Hospital and still suffering from the ordeal she faced in the hospital," I asked.

"We will try, papa, but it is necessary," he said.

"OK, talk to her. It is better that Babli asks her," I suggested.

"Let's try. I already talked to Dr. Ritesh of Kailash Hospital (Dr. Parneesh's brother). He assured that she will get a single room," Babli said.

"Didi, the doctor has advised having a CT, and for that, we have to take you to another hospital," Babli asked her. "We all will be there with you all day and night and not leave you alone this time."

"OK," was the cool reply, which nobody expected.

"I am calling the ambulance," Vicky said.

"Also, please book a ticket for the nurse to go back because we don't know how many days she has to spend in the hospital," I said.

The ambulance arrived, and the security guard was informed.

Laxmi was taken on a stretcher to the ambulance, not knowing that she would never come back.

"Priyanka, please sit with mummy in the ambulance holding her hand the whole way," I said because I had to stay at home with the nurse.

"Sure, papa, please don't worry. I will give you a ring when she is admitted," Priyanka said.

"Take care," I told Laxmi, holding her hand. She nodded.

I was inconsolable after the ambulance moved out. It was so loud that some passersby in the society halted there and asked what happened. I was not aware whether this cry is for Shalu because I never mourn her in front of Laxmi or it is for Laxmi who was again going to the hospital, which I could not tolerate.

"How are you, Masad?" Prerna rang me in the evening.

"I am alright."

"Tomorrow this nurse will also go back. You go to Noida tomorrow," she pleaded.

I don't know why but I nodded. Generally, I don't agree to stay anywhere except our own home.

"Papa, she has been admitted in the Covid ward for tonight until her report of the Covid test comes. She will be shifted to a single room tomorrow after she is tested negative," Vicky informed.

"Is she alright? She should not feel isolated," I asked.

"We are with her here the whole night; you please don't worry," he assured.

"I am not worried but a little scared," I admitted.

"Papa, you agreed to come here tomorrow," he asked.

"Yes, you people never leave any option to me," I said.

Early in the morning, she was shifted to a single room.

"Sharma ji, please come to Noida directly along with the nurse. Our driver will drop her at the station," Manoj's urgent voice echoed through the phone.

"OK, I am coming."

Ultimately, we reached Noida.

"Shall we go to meet didi?" Manoj asked me the next day.

"Yes, I also want to meet her," I said.

"How are you, dear?" I touched her hand after reaching the hospital.

"Don't touch. The doctor has asked not to touch," she said, smiling.

"Let the doctor go to Hell. Nobody can stop me from touching you," I declared.

"Thank God! She is looking good today after a long time," I thought.

"Babli wanted to come with us, but she was getting ready. Shall she come in the evening?" Manoj asked Laxmi.

"Why won't she come? She will come in any case," was the reply in a loud voice. All of us laughed.

We came back with utter satisfaction. She will come home soon. Then a thought immediately came to my mind. How will we tell her about Shalu? I am afraid she might collapse after hearing this news.

"Papa, come early. Mummy had blood vomiting and is unconscious," Vicky cried, calling 2 hours after our return from the hospital.

"What happened?" I asked in a loud voice. Babli came running to me and asked what happened.

I was not in a position to reply and was weeping. Manoj came out of the washroom, and we 3 ran towards the stairs.

"Driver, immediately start the car," was the order.

Within 5 minutes, we reached the hospital.

"Where is Laxmi?" I asked.

She is unconscious, and doctors are trying to revive her.

We ran towards her room. A team of doctors was trying to revive her.

"Sorry, she is no more," they declared after some time.

I kept standing there and could not believe what the doctor said. My whole world was ruined. I reached her and put my hand on her head.

"It's 5 pm. Shall we take her to the cremation directly now?" Manoj asked.

"No, we will go home first. I will inform all my sisters, who wanted to come and meet us after Shalu's demise," I said.

I informed Pushpa Bahanji; we wept on the phone. I requested her to inform everyone. I will inform you about the next programme.

"Hello, Deepak Ji," I called him.

"No, this is Sunder. I heard the news. He is not in a position to talk," he said.

"Please, I want to talk to him," I insisted.

"Hello, I am sorry sir. We all are devastated. I will reach home tomorrow with Krish to bid her bye." And he wept very loudly.

"What happened Jijaji," Ravi entered the hospital with Maanu and Poonam.

"We lost our mother today," he was weeping, hugging me!

"Why didn't you allow me to come and meet her?" he complained.

"We didn't know that this would happen," I said.

We all went to Noida to spend the night and wait for the next day to take her along to our home for the last time.

"Mamaji," "Vinod," "Beta" – everybody hugged me when we reached home with Laxmi, who was waiting for us.

What happened? Why did this happen to us only? They all were weeping profusely. The whole society was gathered there.

"I think we should not get delayed now," somebody said.

"Wait, the barber is coming to cut Vicky's hair, as per ritual, because Vicky has to perform the last rites," I said.

Ultimately, the time had come for all of us to perform the last farewell to my loving wife, the loving mummy of Vicky, Shalu and Priyanka, a lovely sister-in-law of my sisters. Of course, Krish was also standing there in his thoughts after losing his mother and her mother together in a span of 15 days.

We have always been together in good times and bad times. Today you may be leaving this Earth without me, but someday I will meet you there. May God reward you with a peaceful afterlife.

You were the light of my life, and your love still shines in my heart. The memories we shared comfort me every day. Although you are no longer with me in life, I still feel your love. I honour our life together by focusing on the joy we shared. I felt your love every day and still feel you near, loving me. I never wanted to be without you, but your love comforts me. Life without you by my side is possible because I still feel your presence. You left this world, but not my heart. In my grief, my tears give testimony to the love I have for you. I get through each day without you because of the love we shared. Even death did not end our love. Ours was a great love story that we will continue together someday. When we meet again, I shall hold you in my arms and never let you go. Our love was our bond, and even death could not break it. Your death left a gaping hole in my life that I filled with the love we shared. Everything reminds me of you and makes me feel connected to you. I will cherish you forever. You are never out of my heart or thoughts. You may be gone, but I can still see your face and hear your laughter. I shall always love you, even in death. You were more than a wife; you were my best friend. Even though you died, I still feel you near, watching over me. I know that someday we shall be together again.

At last, the time had come to leave her alone at the crematorium, performing the last rites. For the first time, I came back home alone without her.

"Behenji, please sit. I would like to keep my head in your lap and want to take some rest. I am tired Bahanji. I want to sleep," I laid down in the lap of Devi Behenji. For the last more than a month, I got tired of thinking about the health issues of all our family members and wanted to take some rest.

Everything was over. Life had taken a U-turn. We were left alone after doing the kriya of Laxmi. Me – Vicky – Priyanka, a family of 3 persons only.

Today, I want to write you something for both my beloved wife and daughter – with a hope that it may reach you.

"Dearest Shalu & Laxmi,

They say that time is a healer; they say that whatever happens, happens for the best, they say God calls the best person early. But neither time nor this thought that God needs good people, diminishes the painful memories of your departure from our life. It was so sudden that till date we could not believe it, and it seems that you are still there in our life and calling us...

It has been months when God has snatched his marvels from us. It doesn't matter whether it has been weeks, months, or years – the pain of losing people close to your heart will pinch all of us for a lifetime. But one thing is for sure. We always remember the month of May as Black May. We still remember the days spent with you, Shalu when you were a kid, and I started my new life with Laxmi which are the treasures of my life. We never knew that losing members of our family in a spur of the moment would make us feel so aimless, worthless, powerless, heartless, and helpless. I was awfully busy with my work during the time you were grown up, and Laxmi was in the process of converting our house into a home. I haven't been with you both enough, but I have been with you enough to love you and miss you dearly. A bright smile, an endearing voice, a kind heart where compassion dwelt for all beings and animals alike. A life endowed with love, beauty, simplicity, strength, and deep responsibility. Our darling diamonds, our greatest treasure. A precious gift from God just like a light in the dark, forever in our hearts.

It hurts to think that you both are not here anymore. Although we can't help but smile with tears in our eyes to think of how we cherished each and every moment of our lives together when you were with us. Now there is an eerie silence at home...

Wherever you are we just want you to know that no matter how much we've fought and argued, you both were right, is what our heart always knew.

You taught us to be strong but sorry we are letting you down… we can never be strong enough to accept that you are no longer with us.

Death thinks it has taken you away from us, but it doesn't know that it has actually brought us closer than ever.

We want to convey that even though you are not in front of our eyes right now, your picture in our heart will remain beautifully pristine forever. Whether it is the empty spot on the bed or the eerily silent home on a Sunday morning, you are missed in every way, we love you.

Dear both - how heartbroken we are and how much we miss you; we can't explain in words, but our tears do. Sometimes we think we have become so strong when it is about you both but nowadays, we pretend to be, and it always breaks us more.

I am happy, do you know why? Because she left before me. She didn't have to go through the agony and pain of burying me, of being left alone after my departure. I will be the one to go through that, and I thank God. I love her so much that I wouldn't have liked her to suffer...

Your life has ended, but your legacy of wisdom, integrity, and courage will go on forever, we miss you.

A free-spirited person like you can never be proclaimed dead. You may not be around in person, but your spirit will live on forever in our hearts, we miss you.

The best people don't exist in this world. That's because they are in Heaven right now, we miss you.

Just one last chance, we wish we could get to see you both. Then we would hold you tight and never let go. We miss you.

Your Heartbroken Family Members"

A NEW BEGINNING

In the hushed confines of our Mumbai apartment, Vicky's revelation cut through the ordinary rhythm of our lives. "Listen, papa, Priyanka is positive," he confided one day in March 2022. We had made the shift to Mumbai in November 2021 after a series of incidents, an opportunity for Vicky that beckoned us to a new place, a fresh start.

"Oh, when did she get tested?" I inquired.

"Today only," he responded.

"Then she has to be kept in isolation now," I mused, a hint of concern lingering in my voice. Our two-bedroom apartment suddenly felt constrained, limiting a person to just one room posed a logistical challenge.

"What are you thinking, papa? She is pregnant," Vicky dropped another bombshell.

"That's good news," I exclaimed, my joy tempered with a sense of responsibility. A mixed bag of emotions unfurled within me. Priyanka's Pregnancy-positive status brought both elation and trepidation. We had navigated a similar situation before, emerging from the hollow because there was someone there to look after her. But now? Now, there was a big question mark looming over us.

"Please take her to the doctor today itself," I urged. "And take extra care of her this time because it's only the 2 of us who have to handle everything."

"Yes, papa, I am a bit worried."

"Don't worry. God is great," I assured.

At last, the tide turned in our favour. Good news enveloped our home as Priyanka delivered a baby boy. Overwhelmed with gratitude, I stood before the divine, offering thanks for the blessings bestowed upon us.

In the warmth of my signature welcome, I also penned a letter for him: -

"Dear Chhote,

Allow me to bestow upon you this endearing name, for I eagerly await the arrival of another grandson to grant you a more fitting nickname. Until then, let us affectionately call you by this moniker. After all, what significance does a name truly hold? It's you, the essence that matters.

You are the one I long for. The one with whom I wish to share midnight rolls and awaken next to every day for the remainder of my life. The one I am willing to fight for, compromise for, and, if necessary, sacrifice myself for. You are the one with whom I desire to embark on exciting adventures, the one I want to hold during challenging times. You are the one I aim to make happy for the rest of my days. You are the one I never wish to part with or live without. It's you, and only you.

Welcome to this beautiful and enchanting world, which has become even more radiant with your arrival. Thank-you for injecting excitement, amazement, and love into our lives. Your presence has illuminated our world, proving that some of the best things are felt in the depths of our hearts, not merely seen with our eyes.

I understand that, as you read this letter, the nuances may elude you. Perhaps you won't comprehend it fully, or you might struggle to express your emotions. Rest assured; you will grasp the sentiments your grandparents hold for you. We awaited your arrival with bated breath, and though you came a bit later, it seems you are the culmination of the blessings of those who departed while awaiting you.

Perhaps, it feels as if God reserved the best for the last—a celestial gift delivered on angel's wings, a tiny bundle of pure love, the very touch of Heaven on Earth. You are my everything—my world, my friend, my missing piece. I love you more than anything, and I implore you never to leave, for I need you in my life.

My love for you transcends your being; it's for the person I become when I'm with you. It's for the part of me that you unveil and the impact you've had on my life. You've reached into the depths of my heart, transforming the timber of my existence into not just a pub, but a temple. You've done more than any faith could and surpassed any fate in making me happy, all without a touch, a word, or a sign.

You may not fathom your own beauty, but I express my gratitude to God each day for crafting you precisely for me and placing you in my life at an unexpected yet perfect moment.

As you embark on this journey called life, we wish you boundless joy. May your experiences be filled with unending happiness.

Love You the Most,

Dadi and Dadaji"

....

The stagnant clock of our lives, frozen for a while, has now begun to tick and fly. More than a year has passed, witnessing the growth of our beloved Avyaan. Our first and foremost priority is his upbringing as a good person. Now, attempting his first steps, he has evolved into a mischievous bundle of joy. I made a conscious effort to spend most of my time with him; he has become my best friend and the lifeline of our existence. This marks the zenith of our familial bliss — A NEW BEGINNING.